CAPTIVE in the VIRTUAL WORLD

Written by Cathy East Dubowski

Cover Illustration by Greg Winters

Based on the teleplay,
"The Captive" by Robert Hughes

Also based on the teleplay,
"Error in the System" by Mark Litton

PRICE STERN SLOAN
Los Angeles

Creative Consultant: Cheryl Saban
TM and © 1994 Saban Entertainment, Inc. & Saban International N.V.
V.R. TROOPERS and all logos, character names, and distinctive
likenesses thereof are trademarks of Saban Entertainment, Inc., and
Saban International N.V. Used with permission.
Published by Price Stern Sloan, Inc.,
A member of The Putnam & Grosset Group, New York, New York.

Library of Congress Card Catalog Number: 94-68250

ISBN 0-8431-3843-2

First Printing
1 3 5 7 9 10 8 6 4 2

INTRODUCING THE V.R. TROOPERS:

RYAN STEEL

Eighteen-year-old Ryan Steel is the leader of the V.R. TROOPERS. Since the age of nine, Ryan has been training with Grand Master Tao, an expert in teaching discipline, dedication, and spirituality along with the various fighting techniques of karate. Ryan has two burning goals: to become a partner in the dojo and to find his father, Tyler Steel, a physicist and molecular biologist, who disappeared in a freak accident when Ryan was five. Although Tyler Steel has been declared officially dead, Ryan is convinced that his father is still alive—somewhere.

KAITLIN SCOTT

Kaitlin, like Ryan, is in her teens and is also an expert in the martial arts. Kaitlin is strong, athletic, and can keep up with the guys without a problem. She is a hard-hitting photojournalist for a newspaper, the *Underground,* focusing on tough environmental and political issues. She wants to be a reporter to fight Karl Ziktor and the lies he feeds into the media in Cross World City.

J.B. REESE

J.B. is an 18-year-old African American who has been Ryan's best friend since the third grade. They do everything together. J.B. is the group's computer and electronics expert and is as hip as they come. He's highly skilled in the martial arts and his dream is to save enough money to go to college and get a degree in computer engineering.

CHAPTER 1

*E*ighteen-year-old Ryan Steel hung his black helmet on the handlebars of his motorcycle.

Then he walked quietly toward the green and gold temple that glowed in dawn's first blush of color.

He often came here to escape the clogged streets and high-rise buildings of Cross World City. Or to escape the nightmares.

The temple was an oasis of quiet and peace.

A few yards into the courtyard, Ryan bowed to a deep pink and orange sunrise. Then he went through a series of smooth practiced movements. His arms and legs sliced the cool morning air.

"HI-YAH!"

If he squinted, he could almost picture his father still standing there, nodding with approval. The longish dark hair and warm brown eyes. The ready laugh . . .

"You are a good student," tall handsome Tyler Steel had said with a grin. *"A regular chip off the old block."*

He spoke quietly, patiently, as the small, blond Ryan struggled with the karate moves.

There were so many things a man could give his son, Ryan thought now. Material things—but they could break or be lost or stolen. As a scientist, his father could have taught him a great deal about the laws of the universe.

"But facts can be twisted, challenged, shattered," Tyler Steel had told his son. *"Facts alone aren't truth."*

Ryan's father must have wanted to give his only son much more. So he had brought him here to the temple, nearly every day, to practice ancient arts, to learn ancient wisdom. Physical and mental self-discipline. Concentration. Balance. Inner strength. Inner truth.

"Tough lessons for a young man," Tyler Steel had said, ruffling Ryan's blond hair. *"But that's OK. We'll take it step by step, day by day. We've got plenty of time."*

If only his father were here now, Ryan thought—so he could show him how much he'd learned in all these years. If only he could talk to him about the problems he faced.

Tyler Steel had been a brilliant physicist and molecular biologist. But when Ryan was five, his father had disappeared. Vanished mysteriously in a freak laboratory accident, they said.

Ryan had been so young, he never really understood what happened. Only that his father would not be coming back.

The law enforcement agencies of Cross World City agreed. They declared Tyler Steel legally dead. Case closed.

But Ryan didn't care about their documents and declarations. It didn't matter that his father had been missing for more than a decade.

A year ago Ryan had gone to the public library to hunt for the truth. After a long search he had dug up a yellowing copy of the newspaper. His father's handsome face had stared back at him from the front page. The headlines were branded in Ryan's mind: SCIENTIST DISAPPEARS. NO TRACE OF TYLER STEEL.

His father's body had never been found.

That was the fact Ryan clung to.

Somehow, deep in his gut, Ryan believed his father was still alive. And one day—he swore to himself—he would find him.

Ryan closed his eyes as the wind whispered around him, ruffling his hair.

And for a moment he was a young boy again, sending his father an awkward, flying kick.

"I'm training hard, Daddy," Ryan had said. "Nobody's going to be able to mess with me."

His father had laughed out loud at that. Then he added gently, but firmly, "Remember, Ryan. A martial artist never uses his skill unless it's in defense of himself or someone he's protecting."

Ryan had nodded, then showed his father his best move.

"Very good, Ryan," Steel had told his son. "Now let's begin again. . . ."

Ryan reached out to his father—but the image faded. My father was right, Ryan thought, watching the first rays of golden sunlight chasing the dark shadows from the buildings and streets of Cross World City, already clogging with commuters.

But how was I to know that someday I'd have to use all my training to try to save the life of my best friend?

2

CHAPTER

*S*PLASH! Ryan Steel felt like he was crashing into a different world as he dived into the cool, crisp water.

Sounds were different under water, and the body moved under different rules. The water forced you to think about your breathing. About being alive.

He relished the contrast of layered feelings: a soaring sense of freedom. The fear of being trapped in a foreign world.

Ryan glided silently along the blue bottom, scissor-kicking his way around a forest of legs. He pushed as far as he could, testing himself.

At last, lungs burning, he lunged upward

and burst through the surface with a shout. "HI-YA!"

Kaitlin Scott shrieked. *"Ryan!* You . . . !" Words failed her. She responded with well-aimed karate chops to the water.

Ryan threw up his arms against the attack, but he was surrounded.

J.B. Reese drenched him with tidal-wave splashes.

Tao Chung, their karate teacher—their *sensei*—shouted a challenge too. And dunked him from behind.

Ryan tasted chlorine and fumbled in a fog of bubbles. Then his feet found the floor, and he came up sputtering.

Kaitlin and J.B. laughed as Ryan coughed and shook the water from his head. When he'd recovered, he turned to Tao, one eyebrow raised.

His *sensei* held back a smile and bowed ever so slightly, as water dripped from his graying goatee. "In karate—and in pools—always expect the unexpected."

Ryan returned the bow. "I'll remember that," he said. "And, uh . . . same to you," he added with a grin.

Laughing, the four friends drifted to the side of the crowded city pool and climbed out.

At their lounge chairs, another friend waited for them. He wore shades, a T-shirt, a sun visor, and a radio headset. His name was Jeb.

Ryan scratched his friend Jeb behind the ears.

But Jeb—Ryan's reddish-brown bloodhound and constant companion—didn't seem to notice. He was too busy jammin' to music only he could hear.

Ryan laughed and straddled his lounge chair as he dried off with a towel. Crazy dog! Ryan stretched out in the deliciously warm sun and closed his eyes.

Around him he heard ordinary summer sounds. Kids crowded the Cross World City public pool to escape the heat. To hang out with friends. To have good, old, ordinary fun.

These ordinary days helped keep Ryan rooted in reality. Helped him hang on to the knowledge that he was—first and foremost—a normal eighteen-year-old kid.

It helped when the responsibility of his secret seemed too big to keep. Ordinary kids splashing around at a local pool on a hot summer day. That was reality, right?

But Ryan Steel knew the pathway to another reality—virtual reality. A reality created by computers. An artificial world, yet one that contained a powerful threat that could destroy the real world.

Ryan had been inside that virtual reality. And he would never be ordinary again.

*T*ao Dojo. Kaitlin speaking."

That was the phone call that had started it all.

Kaitlin, Ryan, and J.B. had been hanging out at Tao's dojo that day. They had been best friends since they were little kids. All three were students of the martial arts and spent a lot of time working out at the karate school.

Ryan was also a teacher there. He hoped one day to earn enough money to buy into the business and become Tao's partner. Immersing himself in martial arts helped him feel close to his missing father. And he enjoyed passing on to younger kids the lessons his father had taught him.

Tall, athletic Kaitlin plunged into martial arts the same way she did everything: head over heels, and feet first. Though she didn't teach at the school, a lot of young girls who took classes there wished she would. "Girls can do anything!" they argued. "Just look at Kaitlin."

J.B. was helping Tao get the school's business and financial records onto the computer. J.B. was a computer genius. His dream was to go to college and get a degree in computer engineering. But forget the computer-nerd stereotypes from TV and the movies. J.B. was good-looking, into music, and a cool dresser.

So it was not unusual that the three lifelong friends would be at Tao Dojo that afternoon.

But how had a stranger known how to find them there?

"Yes, there's a Ryan Steel here," Kaitlin had said into the phone. Suddenly a strange look passed over her face. "But that's impossible...."

She put her hand over the receiver and looked over at Ryan. "Some guy named Professor Hart is on the phone. He says he has a message from your father."

Ryan and J.B. had both looked stunned.

"My father?" Ryan had said. "My father's been missing for over ten years!"

Ryan had thrown his backpack to the floor and grabbed the receiver with shaking hands. But Professor Hart wouldn't explain anything over the phone. He had asked them all to come to his laboratory right away.

Very strange, the friends had agreed. But Ryan couldn't ignore anything that might help him find his father.

The three friends had driven out of town in Kaitlin's red sports car, with Ryan's dog Jeb asleep in the backseat. On the way there Ryan explained what little he knew about Professor Hart.

"He used to work with my dad," Ryan had said. "I don't really remember him. But from what I've read in back issues of the newspaper, they were really close to some kind of major scientific breakthrough when my dad disappeared."

Eventually they had found their way to a secret laboratory in the mountains.

Once inside, they discovered something amazing.

Professor Alfred Hart was a somewhat eccentric 70-year-old scientist. But he wasn't actually there in the lab.

Instead he spoke to them from a computer screen. "What you're seeing now," he'd explained, "is a holographic digital computer image of me."

That meant he had somehow programmed himself into the computer—so they could talk to him as if he were really there. That was strange enough. But what happened next made talking to a digital old man seem ordinary.

First, Ryan talked to his father. Or at least, a computer image version of him.

The professor had given the three friends special headsets to wear. And Ryan had seen a 30-something Tyler Steel. That was about how old he had been when he disappeared. When Ryan was a little boy. But even though his father was young in the image, this wasn't just an old home video.

"Hello, Ryan," the computer image of his father had said. "Since you're here now, I can only assume something has happened to me."

"Where are you?" Ryan had asked. "Are you alive?"

The image had fluttered then, and he'd gotten no answer. But his father continued.

"In our research, the professor and I have been able to unlock the secret of inter-reality travel. This process allows images created by a computer in virtual reality to pass from that imaginary world into the real world."

J.B. had read about inter-reality travel in science fiction novels. But he didn't know anybody could do it in real life.

"You must listen to the professor," Tyler Steel continued. "Dire circumstances must have arisen for him to have called you. I know you'll make me proud. Good luck, Ryan. I love you."

"I love you, too, Dad," Ryan said. Then the image had disappeared.

Professor Hart had explained to them that there was a mutant in the virtual world. He was an evil being named Grimlord who had also mastered a form of the inter-reality travel technology Tyler Steel had alluded to. With his army of mutant robots, Grimlord planned to break through the reality barrier into the real world. His goal: to conquer the real world.

Then Professor Hart had offered them a choice. He gave each of the teenagers a triangular transformation pendant. These pendants would give them the power and the technology to battle Grimlord's mutant army and save the earth from impending doom.

The choice was theirs.

Ryan could not say no. He knew his father would have wanted him to accept the challenge. Kaitlin and J.B. agreed to join their friend.

With the transformation pendants, the three ordinary teenagers could transform into something completely outrageous: super robotized humans who could travel the super-highways of virtual reality and defend the world from Grimlord's threat.

4

CHAPTER

*R*yan snapped back to the present as somebody popped him on the sole of his foot with a wet beach towel.

"Hey, Ryan," Kaitlin said. "What planet are you on?"

They all laughed. Then Kaitlin caught Ryan's eye. Ryan glanced at J.B. and knew that his two best friends understood. They knew where he'd been. Knew what he'd been thinking of.

Sometimes Ryan wondered if Tao had noticed any change in them. If so, their *sensei* did not show it. It was not easy for Ryan to keep things from his teacher and friend. But for now, at least, their adventures as V.R. Troopers would have to remain a secret.

"So, Tao. Are you glad you came with us?" Ryan asked.

The martial arts master inhaled deeply. "Fresh air. Sunshine. Water. How can I say no?"

Kaitlin smiled as she towel-dried her long hair. "It's good for you to get out of the dojo once in a while and have some fun."

Ryan noticed then that Kaitlin and J.B. were gathering up their gear. "Hey, are you two going somewhere?"

Kaitlin nodded. "The *Underground*."

"Yeah," J.B. added. "Kaitlin promised Woody we'd help install a new graphics program in his computer at the paper." J.B. chuckled. "He's having a little trouble with it."

Kaitlin worked at the newspaper as a photojournalist. Her boss, Woody Stocker, was a hard-hitting editor and investigative reporter. He was a great guy. But he was a little . . . unconventional.

"But you can't leave now," Tao protested. "The fun is just beginning."

Ryan laughed. "J.B.'s idea of a good time is tinkering with a computer."

"Give him a break, guys," Kaitlin said. "Besides, when it comes to computers, Woody needs all the help he can get!"

J.B. tossed Ryan and Tao a little salute as he and Kaitlin headed toward the exit in the chain-link fence. "We'll catch up with you guys later."

Ryan and Tao said good-bye. Jeb was still bopping to the sounds on his headset.

Tao leaned back and closed his eyes. Ryan and his teacher sat quietly for a while. They had been friends for a long, long time. Ryan had begun training with the martial arts master when he was nine years old. The older man was like a father to him now. Tao often lectured him on the power and spirituality of stillness. Meditation. Controlled breathing. He was constantly reminding his student to listen to the music of silence.

The seconds ticked by as Ryan shifted and tried to listen. He breathed in deeply.

Tao cleared his throat and opened one eye in question.

Ryan shrugged. "What do you say, Tao . . . Race me to the end of the pool?"

Tao grinned. "You're on!"

"Ready?" Ryan asked.

"Go!"

They hit the water at the same instant and disappeared.

"Humans," Jeb muttered to himself, shaking the water from his fur. "Get 'em near the water and they act like animals." He thought it was so totally cool being able to talk! He did not know if he would ever get over the thrill.

Lucky break that he'd gone with Ryan and his friends when they'd first met Professor Hart in his secret laboratory.

While the kids were busy talking about computer stuff with the Professor, Jeb had gone exploring. He was a pretty snoopy dog, even for a bloodhound. Sniffing around a weird machine, he had accidentally turned it on.

The lab had rumbled like thunder. Sparks flew. Jeb froze and was completely swallowed up by blinding white light. And the strangest thing happened. Jeb had felt this weird globby bubble in his throat. And before he knew it, he had blurted out:

"Whoaaa! That was *so* intense!"

Famous first words—from a talking dog.

Jeb shook his head and chuckled. Ryan was still not over the shock!

But just wait, Jeb thought. I ain't no novelty act. One day this talking business is going to come in handy.

5

CHAPTER

*C*ross World City was a peaceful but hectic metropolis.

Thousands of glittering high-rise office buildings jutted up into the sky.

People from all over the world clogged the streets and offices, doing business in scores of different languages. And factories struggled to meet those businesses' demands.

But one sinister black building towered many stories above the others. Its top floors almost always seemed enveloped in dark, lightning-laced storm clouds.

23

A dangerous man sat in the executive office at the top of that building. Everyone in Cross World City knew his name: Karl Ziktor.

Ziktor leaned back in his plush executive chair, stroking his pet lizard, Juliet. His office was modern and sleek . . . and cold, very cold.

Everything in the office—the furnishings, the paintings, even Ziktor's clothes—were the most expensive money could buy. Many people would call him a success.

But Ziktor had only just begun. He swiveled his chair around to face the wall of windows behind his desk. He looked down on the rest of the city, and felt a raging hunger in the pit of his stomach. But not for food.

He smiled thinly at his reflection in the smoky glass. "What does a man who already owns half the world desire the most?"

He stroked his lizard and chuckled.

"That's right," he answered himself. "The *other* half."

Someone tapped at the door.

"Come!" he barked. A well-dressed assistant entered and handed him a file. "Mr. Ziktor," he said pleasantly. "Here's the latest computer printout of Ziktor Industries' profit-and-loss statement."

Ziktor didn't bother to thank him. He didn't spare the assistant another glance.

Not surprised, the assistant froze his smile in place and fought the urge to stick out his tongue at Ziktor. Then he backed silently from the room as Ziktor opened the file and began to read.

"Well, well, well, Juliet," he purred to the lizard. "I see our fortunes have grown even greater. Aren't computers wonderful things? They can perform even the most difficult tasks. For good . . . or evil." Ziktor laid Juliet on the polished uncluttered desktop.

Then he reached for what looked like an exotic paperweight. A glass sphere rested on a two-tiered brass base. Ziktor cupped his left hand over the energy sphere. It buzzed like a bug zapper. Red and white lightning bolts shot from the center of the glass.

And Ziktor began to change.

His nasally corporate voice grew slower, deeper . . . like a tape of a voice played too slow in order to frighten children on Halloween.

"Forces of darkness, empower me," Ziktor growled. "Take me back to my virtual reality."

Fingers of lightning snaked up his arm, then pulsed like a crown around his head. His face began to mutate and grow older. Stringy white hair grew down from his scalp. For a moment, he seemed as thin as a skeleton, his skin shriveled and drawn. Like a man who had lived thousands of years.

Then he grew thicker and stronger looking, a stocky warrior, fierce in a helmet and armor. His eyes disappeared into the folds of his leathery face. Beneath a hooked nose, his gash of a mouth turned down in a frown.

This was Karl Ziktor's secret alien form: Grimlord! Master of the virtual world!

He was no longer in his office, but in a strange, dark dungeon. A dungeon that did not exist on earth. Or in space. Or in any time clocked in earth's reality.

This was the darkest gutter of virtual reality, a simulated environment created by computers. But it was computer technology run amok. Its evil surpassed what even science fiction writers could ever imagine.

The cavelike room was crammed with mutant robot creatures. Each one was different from the next in shape and form and color, as if some robot factory had gone haywire.

It would have made a great story, a spine-tingling television show about monsters inside a computer program. Only these computer images could not be flipped off. They could think and act and even slip through holes in the reality barrier.

And they obeyed Grimlord's every word.

Already these mutants had the capability of breaking through a small passage in the reality barrier, passing from their dark universe into the real world.

Grimlord's plan was to eventually find a way to move his entire army from virtual reality into reality. And conquer the entire planet.

When Grimlord suddenly appeared, the startled robots jumped up and down and called his name.

"Hail, Grimlord! Master of the drones!"

"Ah, my mechanized mutants," Grimlord called from his throne. "You far outshine mere mortals with your powers."

The robots clapped and cheered.

Grimlord basked for a moment in their adoration.

But Grimlord, like Karl Ziktor, was impatient. And his business in the virtual world was even more urgent. He motioned for silence. Then he ordered: "I call upon Iceborg to update me on the development of my latest technology."

Lightning shot from Grimlord's wand, and the image of his underling floated on a screen above their heads.

"Your report, Iceborg!"

"Your Lordship!" Iceborg answered obediently. "We are making great progress on our plans to penetrate the computers in the real world."

Grimlord nodded his approval.

"One of our devices is almost completed. It will allow you to take anyone captive through a computer terminal and hold him prisoner— here, in virtual reality."

"Well done, Iceborg!" Grimlord's chuckle rumbled like thunder. "And my first victims will be the V.R. Troopers!"

The mutants roared their approval.

"Once they are out of the way"—Grimlord rubbed his hands in anticipation—"no one will be able to stop us. We will totally conquer their reality!"

6 CHAPTER

*K*aitlin Scott shoved through the doors of the *Underground.*

As always, her heart quickened in the newsroom. This is where her dreams of being a hard-hitting photojournalist had begun.

As a photographer, Kaitlin looked at the world in a special way. She strongly believed that the camera could often capture truths that mere words could not. And she wanted to spend her life uncovering those truths.

Most of the other reporters seemed to be out this afternoon, covering stories. That or taking an extra long lunch! Kaitlin grinned and dumped her backpack on her desk. Then she led J.B. to an office in the corner.

A man of about forty, wearing a football helmet, sat at a computer. He shouted and mumbled under his breath as he bobbed and weaved in front of the screen.

"Um, excuse us, Woody," Kaitlin said. "Are you busy?"

Woody Stocker, editor of the *Underground*, grinned. But his eyes stayed glued to the screen. "Check it out!" he said through his face mask. "This is my new football computer game. I'm going for my highest score." He hammered the keys with his forefingers. "I'm on the forty, the thirty . . . I'm going all the way! *Touchdown*! All right!" Woody spiked his keyboard as he jumped to his feet. His chair crashed to the floor. "Ooops!" He looked at Kaitlin and J.B. sheepishly. "Sometimes I get a little too excited."

J.B. just grinned and stuck out his hand. "I came by to help out with your new software installation. Kaitlin said you were having a little trouble."

"Wonderful idea!" Woody chirped. "Great! Thanks!" But instead of shaking hands, he clutched a dictionary to his ribs, posed like a football player, then stiff-armed his way out of the office.

Kaitlin rolled her eyes and J.B. laughed. Then he sat down at Woody's computer. "Let me see what I can do."

"Great," Kaitlin said. "I've got a photo spread to work on. Let me know if I can help."

She went over to a nearby layout table and soon lost herself in her pictures.

Like a pilot slipping into the cockpit, J.B. pulled up his seat and reached for the controls. "Now, let's see what we've got here. . . ."

Deep in the virtual world, Grimlord's temper was coming to a slow boil. Things were happening far too slowly to please him. In a huff, he stabbed his wand in the air and projected his floating screen onto the dark dungeon walls.

"Iceborg!" Grimlord shouted. "I grow impatient. Report!"

Iceborg's image filled the screen. "I've done it, Your Lordship!"

An excited murmur passed through the mob of mutant robots. They crushed closer to see.

"Let me hear your good news," Grimlord said. "And don't leave out a single detail!"

That made Iceborg stutter a little at the beginning of his report. "Well, Your Lordship, that is, uh . . . *one* of our projects has been completed."

Grimlord frowned. "Explain!"

"We are very, very close to success with the computer virus project," Iceborg said. "Truly, I expect a breakthrough any day now."

A low growl began rumbling in Grimlord's chest. This was not such good news. "What about the other project, then?"

"That's the big news," Iceborg happily reported. "Your computer captivation device is now ready to go on-line."

"Excellent!" Grimlord cried.

Iceborg closed his eyes with a relieved sigh.

"And," Grimlord continued, "I know exactly where I want you to use it first. Listen closely. Here is what I want you to do."

J.B.'s hands flew over the keyboard. He was barely aware of Woody's office, he was so caught up in his work.

To J.B. Reese, diving into complex computer problems was like detective work. He continued working methodically, eliminating the possibilities one by one. At last a smile spread across his face. "There!" He sat back in his chair. "I think I've corrected the problem."

J.B. stood up to find Woody. Suddenly the words on the computer screen seemed to melt into a dark blob.

J.B. peered closer. "Huh?"

The blob turned into a face. Iceborg's face!

"Kaitlin!" J.B. shouted. "Check it out!"

Kaitlin dropped her photo wheel and hurried into Woody's office. "J.B., what's going on?"

But before her friend could speak, Iceborg announced in a chilling robotic voice from the computer: "His Highness, Grimlord, requests your presence in his dungeon."

J.B. frowned. "Yeah, right. Fat chance you'll ever find me going there!"

Iceborg scoffed, "I'm afraid you have no choice."

J.B. froze as a cloud of electrical energy surged from the computer screen. Kaitlin and J.B. stared at it, speechless. Then like a giant ghostly hand, it seized J.B.

Kaitlin gasped. She grabbed for J.B.'s arm. But it was too late.

J.B. was sucked into the computer!

7

CHAPTER

J.B.!" Kaitlin cried, horrified. Without thinking, she clawed at the screen. The flat smooth glass was cold against her palms. "J.B.! Come back!"

A face began to emerge. But it wasn't her friend's. It was the terrifying face of Iceborg!

Kaitlin jerked her hands to her chest as his eyes bored into hers. "Kaitlin. Step closer, my dear. You're next!"

With a shout, Kaitlin snapped off the computer and stumbled back against the wall. Trembling, she stared at the screen. It was black. Iceborg was gone. And so was J.B.!

"Hey, where's J.B.?" Woody said as he bopped back into the office. "Did he finish already?" He looked around and scratched his head. "Gosh, he must have left here in a flash."

"You . . . you might say that." Kaitlin took a deep breath to calm herself. She felt like screaming. Instead, she drew on her martial arts training to take control of her emotions. To concentrate. Her fear was a stumbling block that she must overcome. What was important now was clear thinking. Action. How would she save J.B.?

"Uh, listen, Woody. I gotta go. See you." Kaitlin grabbed her backpack as she dashed from the newsroom. Heart pounding, she tossed her bag into the backseat of her red convertible sports car and leapt over the door into the driver's seat. She pulled out into the flowing traffic.

A few minutes later, Kaitlin's car was stuck in a traffic jam. If only she could just go flying off over the tops of the other cars! Pounding the steering wheel with her palms, she looked around impatiently.

All around her she saw ordinary people doing ordinary things. Listening to the news on their way home from work. Heading to a restaurant to have dinner with friends. Crossing the street to the grocery store.

Kaitlin gripped the wheel and willed the traffic to move. "If they only knew . . ." she whispered. Their happy ordinary lives were in danger of being ripped apart. Only one thing stood between them and that nightmare.

The power of the V.R. Troopers!

At last the traffic moved. Kaitlin had a madman to stop. She had a life to save. If only she could find out where that life had gone.

Ryan and Tao had returned to the dojo. Relaxed from their afternoon of swimming and goofing off, they were now practicing a T'ai Chi exercise together.

Ryan's movements mirrored those of his teacher. Their motions were slow, smooth, controlled, as if they moved to a music only they could hear. Finally the exercise ended. Teacher and student bowed slightly to each other.

"That was good, Ryan."

"Thanks, *sensei.*"

"Care to join me in some herbal tea I have prepared?" Tao asked. "It is very nutritious.

Very strengthening. Might even make you stronger than Tao," he added with a twinkle in his eye.

"No, thanks," Ryan said with a grin. Tao was always concocting new recipes that he claimed would improve their martial arts skills. He experimented with herbs and other ingredients. Sometimes the experiments tasted great. Other times . . .

"I think I'll head for home," Ryan said.

Tao bowed again. "See you tomorrow."

After Tao went home, Ryan stretched out a little more. Then he collected his things and headed for the exit—just as Kaitlin rushed in, breathless.

"Ryan! Something terrible has happened!"

"What is it?" Ryan asked. "What's wrong?"

Kaitlin gulped some air, then looked at Ryan with fear-filled eyes. "It's J.B."

"What's happened?" Ryan was instantly worried. He and J.B. had been friends since third grade.

Kaitlin's words rushed out: "He was pulled into the world of virtual reality . . . through Woody's computer . . . by one of Grimlord's robots."

"Whoa, slow down," Ryan said, his head spinning. "Are you saying J.B. is being held inside a computer?!"

Kaitlin shook her head. "I—I'm not sure where they took him."

"We've got to contact Professor Hart."

Kaitlin nodded. "The V.R. disk!"

Kaitlin and Ryan ran to the computer in the dojo office. Ryan pulled a disk from his backpack. Professor Hart had given it to them. With it they could communicate with the scientist from any computer. Ryan jammed the disk into the disk drive.

A face appeared immediately. But it wasn't the gentle face of Professor Hart. It was Iceborg!

"Well, hello, again, Troopers!" the alien robot greeted them.

Kaitlin grabbed Ryan's arm. "Quick, Ryan! Shut it down!"

Ryan hit the keys and ejected the disk. Kaitlin flicked off the machine.

The two friends stared numbly at the computer. The screen was black. Only their own worried faces stared back at them from the reflection in the glass.

"Iceborg! You fool!" Grimlord was furious. His voice shook the walls of his virtual dungeon. "You should have had them!"

"It's not my fault," Iceborg whined.

"Enforcer!" Grimlord shouted. "Send in a squad of skugs to bring the Troopers to me."

"At once," the Enforcer said with a bow.

Kaitlin let out the breath she was holding and plopped down into a chair. She'd almost gone computer diving—for the second time that day!

"That's exactly what happened before J.B. disappeared. That same face showed up on the computer at the paper. J.B shouted for me to come see, and the next thing I knew"—she looked forlornly at Ryan—"he was sucked right into the screen."

Ryan clutched the edge of the desk, thinking. "We've got to find out where they've taken him."

"Right," said Kaitlin. "But where in the world do we start?"

Suddenly the front door to the dojo opened and slammed. Kaitlin and Ryan looked up.

Three men in *gis* walked across the main room and silently filed into the office.

"I'm sorry," Ryan said politely. "The dojo is closed."

The men did not speak. Nor did they leave.

Ryan frowned. "Uh, maybe you could come back another time. Would you like a brochure about our classes?"

Ryan and Kaitlin covered their faces as three flashes lit up the room and the three men changed into three skugs!

"Uh, maybe not," Kaitlin quipped, jumping up from her chair.

She and Ryan split up. They automatically went into a karate stance and faced the intruders.

Ryan blocked the assault of one skug as another lunged for Kaitlin. The third tried to maneuver around in the small office to get Ryan from behind.

Kaitlin struck her skug with a flying kick. Then she leaped over the desk to protect Ryan's back from the third. "HI-YAH!"

Ryan and Kaitlin were outnumbered, but Tao's training served them well. Their motions were well rehearsed, their skills ingrained deeply into their subconscious.

Their defensive actions were a reflex, almost as natural as breathing.

Finally Ryan grabbed two skugs. Kaitlin captured the other. They slammed the mutants into each other and the skugs disappeared in a flash of sparks.

Ryan and Kaitlin looked around a moment, still on guard, hands raised in a defensive stance.

"You OK?" Ryan asked Kaitlin.

"Yeah, I'm all right," she said.

"Looks like Grimlord won't be happy until he captures us, too."

"We need the professor's help," Kaitlin said.

Ryan shook his head. "Reaching him on the computer is definitely out. I say we go to the lab. Come on."

They grabbed their backpacks and raced outside. Every minute counted now. Every second could be J.B.'s last.

*F*ools! All of you!" Grimlord's voice shook into the darkest corners of his virtual world. "I should have had those Troopers—here, now!"

His robot soldiers trembled, rattling their miscellaneous parts. They muttered and groaned their agreement to whatever their master said. Amidst the robot voices, one human voice spoke up. It was weak but clear.

"You'll never capture them. They're way too smart for you."

Grimlord turned his eyes toward the speaker. Ah, what a delight to look upon his prisoner!

J.B. hung limply, locked in a glowing electronic field. J.B. glared at the evil master, and Grimlord grinned, pleased to see his prisoner awake. "Welcome to my reality, Trooper. Virtual reality, of course."

J.B. took a deep breath and answered, "You can't get away with this, Grimlord!"

"Who's going to stop me?" Grimlord smirked. "Surely not you."

J.B. struggled against his bonds, trying to lash out at his captor. But though he saw no chains, no ropes, he could not move. Beads of sweat broke out on his forehead. He felt ill and weak. "What's happening to me?" he gasped.

"Enforcer!" Grimlord shouted. "Explain his fate to him."

"You are Grimlord's captive. He is slowly draining you of your power to become a V.R. Trooper. Once he has captured that power, he will channel the energy into his drones, who will take over your reality." The Enforcer seemed to take a great deal of pleasure in his little speech.

"That's impossible," J.B. said.

"Oh, is it?" Grimlord asked with a sneer. His hand swept the air as if swatting a pesky mosquito. Instantly the energy field around J.B. burned brighter.

J.B. muffled a groan and slumped.

"Feeling weaker?" Grimlord asked with a hearty laugh. "Soon you will be drained of all your powers. And then, using my new computer device, I will add two new Troopers to my collection."

Grimlord's general, Battlebot, blurted out eagerly, "And when you do, it will be my honor to destroy them for you, Your Lordship."

The rowdy mutant robots cheered.

J.B. shook his head and struggled in his invisible electronic bonds. I've got to fight them, he thought. Can't let them get to me . . . can't let them win! Then he stilled himself. This was no time to panic. He must draw on his logic. Make plans. He wasn't sure how quickly his powers were being drained. But he knew he must save his strength.

J.B. slowly surveyed this strange, cavelike place. He couldn't quite tell how many of these weird robots there were; it was too dark. But darkness could be an advantage to an escaping prisoner.

He knew he was outnumbered, of course. But these guys didn't look very smart. Timing and the right moves could go a long way. How did these creatures come and go here?

There! In the far corner, hidden by darkness and smoke, was a door. If he could somehow get to that door and escape. But what was on the other side?

Well, it couldn't be worse than what's in here, he reminded himself, deciding to rest. And he would keep his eyes and ears open. Grimlord was quite a braggart. J.B. might be able to learn something while he was here that would help the Troopers in their struggle against this virtual army.

He clung to one thought. Sooner or later he'd have a chance to escape. He must be ready for that moment. He had to believe that that moment would come. He had to believe that somehow his friends would come for him.

If they could find him.

9

CHAPTER

*R*yan and Kaitlin yanked on helmets, jumped onto Ryan's motorcycle, and zoomed out of Cross World City.

Soon the towering, glass-and-steel high-rises were far behind them. Cement and smog were replaced by trees and fields and fresh air. They had made this trip to Professor Hart's secret laboratory many times before. But never had the winding road seemed to go on for so long.

Finally they came to a familiar spot. Ryan and Kaitlin leaned into the turn. The bike kicked up gravel as they veered off the main road.

At last! In the distance they spotted their final landmark. The bridge. The lab was just on the other side. Ryan flew over the bridge and skittered the bike to a stop.

He and Kaitlin jumped off, and Ryan quickly hid the bike among the trees. Then they hurried the last few steps into the woods until they saw the door to the lab.

Ryan would never forget how strange it had looked the first time they had all seen it. It was a tepee-shaped blue door set into a doorframe—and nothing else—standing in the middle of nowhere.

That first time they had been terrified of crossing the threshold. How could they have guessed what was on the other side? But that was before they became V.R. Troopers. Now they often sprinted into the unknown.

This time when the door whooshed open, Ryan and Kaitlin strode through without a second thought. They seemed to disappear as the blue door slammed shut behind them.

But they had actually entered the mysterious world of Professor Hart's secret lab. The one he had shared with Ryan's father, Tyler Steel, so many years ago.

"Professor Hart! We need your help!" Kaitlin cried.

The large ultra-modern lab—ceiling, walls, floor, equipment—was almost entirely white. The only color came from the black rectangular control panels around the room which lit up with blinking colored lights.

Jeb had been curled up asleep, but he jumped to his paws as his friends ran in. "What about me?" he said sleepily. "What am I, chopped liver?"

"It's no joke, Jeb," Ryan answered his dog. "Grimlord has captured J.B."

In the center of the room was a console, with a computer keyboard and a monitor. On the screen they saw the slightly rumpled head and shoulders of Professor Alfred Hart appear.

Professor Alfred Hart was not really there, however. What they were actually seeing was a holographic digital computer image of the man. The professor may have only existed on their computer monitor, but he was a genius problem solver who was able to access and monitor the virtual world.

In the high-tech lab, the scientist looked a little nerdy. But even rumpled and a little eccentric—even though he was well into his seventies—Professor Hart had a brilliant mind. And a kind heart, too. Ryan and Kaitlin knew that if anyone could help them save J.B., he could.

"What?" Professor Hart asked. "Grimlord? Captured J.B., you say? How is this possible?"

"He was sucked into my computer at the newspaper," Kaitlin said. "He just vanished!"

"Hmm . . ." Professor Hart seemed to lose his train of thought for a moment. But the kids knew to wait patiently. It just meant he was thinking. Professor Hart's face moved in closer, filling the screen. "Undoubtedly Grimlord is holding J.B. in a virtual prison."

Ryan ran his hand through his short blond hair. "But where?"

"Yes, well . . . perhaps it's time for a little computer spy work," Professor Hart said.

"Wait!" Ryan cried. "If we use your computer screen, we risk the chance of getting captured ourselves."

"Eh? Oh . . ." Professor Hart shook his head. "No, no, no, no. I was going to suggest traveling through virtual reality. Please put on your V.R. visors."

"Hey!" Jeb yelped and scuttled over to the screen. "I want in on this action, too."

Ryan helped his dog put on his shiny visor. Even under serious conditions like these, it was hard not to laugh at how crazy the talking dog looked. Especially when he began to run wildly around the lab, chasing the images the visor allowed him to see.

Kaitlin was always surprised at how light-weight the curved, one-piece visors were. Tiny red lights blinked across the top, as the microchips worked their computerized magic. There was a wide narrow black band across the eye area. The wearers didn't look *through* these visors, but deep *into* computerized images.

These inventions were the pathway to the secret Ryan's father had discovered right before he disappeared. With these visors Ryan and his friends could experience inter-reality travel. This process allowed virtual reality images to pass from the virtual world to the real world on earth.

Ryan and Kaitlin picked up their visors and put them on. And they both gasped at what they saw.

*R*yan's and Kaitlin's vision instantly changed. Now they bobbed and weaved and waved their arms to keep their balance as they seemed to rush down a wildly twisting tunnel of bright carnival lights.

They had worn these visors many times before. But each time it was still a mind-blowing experience.

"Wow, Professor!" Ryan cried, fascinated. "What are we seeing?"

Professor Hart chuckled. "We're tracing the fiber optic transmission route that links the computer at Kaitlin's paper with the source of J.B.'s captors."

"Wow," Jeb broke in, swaying dizzily. "Welcome to the barf zone!"

"Is it much farther, Professor?" Kaitlin asked.

"You're nearly there," the professor replied.

Suddenly the tunnel of colored light ended.

Ryan and Kaitlin still had their feet planted firmly on the polished white floor of the lab. They still wore their visors. But to them it seemed as if they had entered a dark, smoky dungeon. A mob of mutant robots of all shapes and designs mingled before a sinister-looking throne.

"Check this out," Ryan whispered. "It's Grimlord's dungeon."

Kaitlin suddenly grabbed Ryan's arm. "Look! There's J.B.!"

J.B. hung motionless in the glowing electric field that held him prisoner. He looked tired and weak. Even so, his face looked defiant.

"Oh, my," Professor Hart murmured. "He's being held in some sort of immersive electronic field."

"But why doesn't he just transform, Professor?" Ryan demanded helplessly. "As a V.R. Trooper he could fight these creatures."

"He can't," the Professor answered. "The immersive electronic field has deenergized his virtualizer. He's trapped."

They watched as Grimlord pounded the arm of his throne with his fist. He looked extremely unhappy.

"My skugs are worthless," they heard Grimlord complain. "How could they have possibly failed to capture the other Troopers?"

"Excuse me, Your Lordship?" the Enforcer asked. "What shall we do with our prisoner?"

Grimlord's wrinkled face mushed into what almost looked like a smile. "Finish draining his virtual energy," he ordered. "Then let Battlebot destroy him!"

Ever ready to grovel, Grimlord's mutant robots cheered their master's command. They shook their weapons and hollered insults at the prisoner.

J.B. wished he could move his hands to cover his ears and block their cheering. But he raised his chin and bravely glared back at his captors. He would show no fear.

Grimlord howled with laughter. What good sport this all was!

Back in Professor Hart's lab, Kaitlin and Ryan slowly removed their V.R. visors.

What had seemed so real—what had seemed to be happening right here before them—instantly disappeared. It was as if someone had clicked off a TV. They stared at each other in horror for a moment, not speaking.

"We've got to do something!" Kaitlin cried at last. "We've got to act fast!"

Ryan nodded in agreement, his mind racing. "If we don't get to J.B. right away," he said, "we might lose him forever."

I'm going in after him!"

Kaitlin stopped her pacing and stared at her good friend Ryan as if he were a stranger. "What did you say?"

"I'm going in after him," Ryan repeated.

"That's very brave of you, Ryan," Professor Hart said gently. "But I'm afraid your powers as a V.R. Trooper will not allow you to access Grimlord's dungeon in virtual reality."

Ryan and Kaitlin continued to pace.

Jeb followed them back and forth. The faithful dog wanted to do his part. And humans seemed to think that this zigzag walking would somehow help.

Then Ryan's head shot up. "What if I let him take me captive?"

"Ryan!" Kaitlin exclaimed. "What are you saying?"

Ryan's brown eyes darted back and forth as he came up with a plan. "I transform here in the lab," he explained. "Then we activate the computer screen—with me in front of it—and let Grimlord's henchmen pull me through to his virtual reality dungeon."

Professor Hart nodded thoughtfully. "It just might work."

Kaitlin held up her hands and shook her head. "No way! That's totally crazy, Ryan. It would be you against Grimlord's entire army of mutant robots."

But Ryan's mind was already made up. There simply was no time for group discussion or alternative plans. He had to act now.

"If the tables were turned and I was the prisoner . . . I know J.B. would come after me," Ryan said.

"I'm going with you, then," Kaitlin insisted.

"No," Ryan said. "You'll be more help here in the lab with Professor Hart."

"But—"

"No, Kaitlin." Ryan's voice was quiet but firm. "Look, I need you here. To monitor my progress and give me some backup if I call for help."

"You know, he's right, Kaitlin," Professor Hart added gently.

Kaitlin hesitated. She hated sitting on the sidelines. She was never one to resist a challenge, and she never backed off from an important fight. How could they ask her to do that now, when something as important as her friend's life was on the line? Waiting was far tougher than taking decisive action.

Kaitlin started to protest again. But she stopped when she stared into Ryan's level gaze. She and Ryan had been friends since they were kids, and she knew that look. Nothing in the world would be able to change his mind now. She might as well save her energy. Besides, she admitted, she and Ryan and J.B.—plus Professor Hart and Jeb—were a team. And the plain truth was that only teamwork would get J.B. out of this life-threatening situation.

"OK," she said at last. "I'll stay here. And I'll be here for you, Ryan. Every second you're gone. But be careful." She smiled softly. "Get yourself and J.B. back safely. OK?"

Ryan nodded then stepped back. He took out his triangular transformation pendant. The glowing virtualizer would give him the power to become a V.R. Trooper. Then he could face Grimlord and his mutant robots. On their own turf. On their own terms.

Not a fair fight by any means, he thought grimly. But it's the only shot I've got.

Ryan gave Kaitlin a lopsided grin.

She answered with a thumbs-up.

Then his face became a mask of concentration as he turned to his task.

He raised the pendant high—and the room was bathed in a shocking red glow. "Trooper transform!" Powerful blue lightning rocketed from the pendant's core. A sound like electronic feedback on an amplifier rang in their ears. And Ryan transformed in a shattering of colored light. Two yellow eyes glowed from a silver face. The transformation was complete.

Gone was the ordinary teenager. In his place was Ryan, the V.R. Trooper, a powerful high-tech champion—the living manifestation of Tyler Steel's virtual reality discoveries.

Jeb looked at his master in total admiration. "I wish I could do that," he mumbled.

Kaitlin sighed. She wished she were going with Ryan.

V.R. Ryan stepped up to the computer. "Now," he said. "Time to set out the bait." He took a deep breath, then activated the screen. At first the standard menu appeared. But then the images on the screen began to crawl like electronic worms. Seconds later Iceborg's face took over the screen.

"Hello again," he said, his robotic voice laced with a bit of surprise. "What's this? Decided to tempt fate, Trooper?"

"We're not afraid of you or your kind," V.R. Ryan stated boldly.

Iceborg grunted a laugh. "You should be."

Kaitlin fought for control, to keep from yanking V.R. Ryan back from danger. She'd already lost one friend this way today. To stand back and willingly let another one go took all the strength she could muster.

V.R. Ryan stood firm as he allowed a pulsing glow to surround him. It felt like giant fingers. He felt every atom in his body quivering. Then in an instant he was sucked into the screen.

Kaitlin rushed to the computer. Her hand reached out—and froze.

Do it! she commanded herself. Do it now! And she shut the computer down. She knew her friend couldn't see her or hear her. But that didn't matter. She spoke to him anyway.

"Good luck, Trooper Ryan!" She stared into the blank screen as if it were a dark tunnel, as if she might catch one last glimpse of him. "Go get J.B. and bring him home!"

Then Kaitlin began the greatest challenge she'd faced as a V.R. Trooper. She sat down to wait.

12

CHAPTER

Virtual Reality Ryan felt the rush of crashing into a different world. He looked straight ahead as he was sucked down another wildly twisting tunnel of bright lights.

He was traveling the fiber optic transmission route that linked the computer in Professor Hart's labs to J.B.'s captors. It was exciting to soar so freely. But the tingle of fear at diving into the hands of an enemy sent his blood pumping. Mentally he was ready to face whatever lay ahead.

As he raced along, he thought briefly of his father. Of the lessons that had first taken root in his mind during martial arts training sessions.

His mind replayed his father's words:

"Remember, Ryan. A martial artist never uses his skill unless it's in defense of himself or someone he's protecting."

V.R. Ryan felt as if all his training for all those years had been in preparation for this moment. His best friend was in trouble. And V.R. Ryan had a chance to save his life.

He also recalled the advice Professor Hart had once given the Troopers. J.B. had asked if there was anything they could do to stay ready for Grimlord and his army.

"Of course," the professor had answered. "Practice your martial arts. The more you sharpen your skills, the more effective your special powers will be."

That was the easy part. Tao was a strict teacher. Sure, he had his fun side. But when it came to martial arts, the *sensei* believed in discipline. He inspired Ryan to constantly strive for perfection.

Fine lessons from three excellent teachers, V.R. Ryan thought. Their teachings had become a part of him. He concentrated on the end of the tunnel. He felt prepared.

THUNK! V.R. Ryan landed on his feet as the wild ride unexpectedly ended. He shook his head and looked around, trying to get his bearings.

There! He was only steps away from J.B.! But his friend was still trapped in a strange web of glowing electricity. V.R. Ryan rushed to his friend's side. "J.B.! Are you OK?"

But Grimlord's sluggish voice answered for him. "I'm afraid your friend is feeling a bit . . . drained."

V.R. Ryan crouched in closer to hear J.B. whisper: "Trooper Ryan! Hey . . . thanks for coming." Then J.B. shook his head in disgust. "They've sapped my strength."

V.R. Ryan looked directly into his friend's brown eyes and said with complete confidence, "I'm gonna get you out of here, buddy."

"Oh, really?" Grimlord bellowed, obviously eavesdropping. "You and what army, Steel?"

Trooper Ryan spun around. He glared up at his enemy sitting so calmly on his throne.

Grimlord clucked. "Face it, Steel. You and your friend are doomed."

Keeping his eyes on his surroundings, V.R. Ryan whispered to J.B. "Have you seen a way out of here?"

J.B. nodded almost imperceptibly toward a dark corner. "There's a portal over there," he whispered.

Peering into the smoky gloom, V.R. Ryan spotted the door. He nodded a fraction of an inch.

"I have patiently awaited this moment," Grimlord continued to rant. "And now your total destruction is at hand."

V.R. Ryan looked his adversary in the eye. "Don't count me out yet, Grimlord."

Grimlord's tsk-tsked and shook his head. "Overconfident," he sneered. "Just like your father."

"Hey!" V.R. Ryan cried out. He jumped to his feet. "What do you know about my dad?"

"He was weak . . . like you," Grimlord said smugly. "No match for my powers."

Grimlord's sick chuckles rolled down on V.R. Ryan like an avalanche of jagged rocks. "He was easy prey."

"You slimy mutant!" V.R. Ryan yelled. "Where is he? What did you do to him?" He charged through the throng of jabbering robots and lunged for Grimlord on his throne.

The evil dictator raised his wand, firing a golden bolt of light. It struck V.R. Ryan in the chest, tumbling him backward into the crowd.

V.R. Ryan stumbled, but quickly rolled to his feet. "It'll take more than that to stop me!" he shouted.

"Aaaghh!" Grimlord grunted, throwing up his hands. "Finish them off! Battlebot, I leave you in charge."

Trooper Ryan charged the throne again. But Grimlord vanished in a burst of blue and red sparks.

Coward! V.R. Ryan thought angrily. He talks big. Then he leaves his underlings to do his dirty work.

All of Grimlord's army stared at the empty throne for a moment as the last sparks and wisps of smoke disappeared.

V.R. Ryan wasted no time missing the evil leader. Thinking quickly, he charged toward Battlebot and snatched his sword.

"Hey!" a stunned Battlebot blurted out.

But Trooper Ryan turned his sights on the Enforcer. "Come on, you refugee from the junkyard," he taunted the robot. "Let's see how tough you really are."

Startled, the Enforcer paused for a moment, eyeing his opponent. Then he chuckled and raised his own sword in answer to Ryan's challenge. "Gladly!" the Enforcer cried.

The mob of mutant robots gathered round eagerly, as if witnessing a playground fight between a bully and his victim.

Too bad there wasn't a principal to break up the fight. Because V.R. Ryan suddenly had a sinking feeling.

In this fight he was definitely outnumbered.

V.R. Ryan and the Enforcer faced off. Their swords clanged, and clanged again, as they matched each other, strike for strike.

Just like a scene from the *Three Musketeers*, V.R. Ryan thought, as a strange bubble of laughter caught in his throat. Only this time the other two Musketeers were counting on him to pull the whole thing off.

By the looks of the Enforcer's clumsy swordplay, V.R. Ryan thought, I don't think he's practiced enough.

With his years of defensive martial arts training behind him, V.R. Ryan held his own against the Enforcer.

"Way to go, Trooper Ryan," J.B. called out weakly.

V.R. Ryan pushed forward, pressing the Enforcer toward the wall. With a sudden move, he knocked the Enforcer's sword from his hand. It clattered as it tumbled across the rocky dungeon floor. The Enforcer seemed stunned.

V.R. Ryan seized the moment to race back to his friend through the jeering mob. Several robots attacked him, and he tossed the mutants left and right. A flying kick sent another one flying into the shadows.

"J.B.," V.R. Ryan called as he fought off his attackers. "You ready to get out of here, man?"

"I'm not sure I can make it," J.B. answered.

V.R. Ryan downed a robot with a well-aimed kick. Then he rushed to his friend's side. "Come on, J.B. You can do it!"

V.R. Ryan sunk his transformed hand into the force field imprisoning his buddy. He grabbed J.B.'s flesh-and-blood hand and pulled. Using all his powers, V.R. Ryan yanked him out.

J.B. tumbled free with a loud sucking sound, like a giant foot being pulled from thick mud.

The force field shimmered . . . and disappeared.

J.B. slumped into V.R. Ryan's arms. "Thanks," he gasped, shaking his head. "I owe you."

"Come on, buddy," V.R. Ryan encouraged him. "I'm getting you out of here."

Trooper Ryan wrapped one of J.B.'s arms across his shoulders, then rushed him toward the exit.

The dull-witted mutants scrambled in the confusion V.R. Ryan left in his wake. "After them, you fools!" the Enforcer cried.

V.R. Ryan and J.B. struggled out through the door. They fled into the forest that surrounded Grimlord's headquarters. But after only a few steps J.B. staggered at V.R. Ryan's side.

"Come on, J.B.," V.R. Ryan encouraged his friend. "Keep going. You can make it."

Behind them they heard Battlebot shouting to Grimlord's army: "There they go! Fire upon them!"

A moment of silence. Then *BOOM!* Grimlord's cannonbots exploded. Hunks of rock and splintered trees showered V.R. Ryan and J.B. as they ran.

Then J.B. stumbled to the ground. V.R. Ryan knelt quickly and examined his friend.

71

J.B. was exhausted. He wouldn't be able to go much farther.

V.R. Ryan glanced back over his shoulder.

Grimlord's mutant army was bearing down on them.

"Go ahead, Trooper Ryan," J.B. cried. "Run!" He stopped to gasp for breath. Then he looked up into his best friend's eyes and pleaded, "Hurry! Save yourself!"

CHAPTER 14

Kaitlin paced impatiently across the floor of Professor Hart's lab. Jeb's paws clicked on the floor as he followed her. She paced back toward the portal. Jeb clicked along at her heels. Back and forth. Back and forth she went.

"Aaagh! He's been gone too long!" Kaitlin cried out impatiently.

"Chill out," Jeb said. He stopped long enough to chomp an itch on his left shoulder. "Listen, Trooper Ryan is awesome. He can take care of himself."

"Kaitlin," Professor Hart suddenly called. "Come quickly. I'm picking up a signal from sector 4."

Kaitlin dashed to the monitor. At first all she saw was dense forest. Then . . . there! She saw two figures—human figures—crouched within the trees. "Hey, look! Ryan's got J.B!"

"Yeah," Jeb said, and he began to growl ferociously. "But look who's behind them."

Grimlord's airbots screamed through the air by threes, peppering the ground with gunblasts.

On the ground below, V.R. Ryan still knelt beside his friend. He gave J.B. a moment to catch his breath, to pull himself together. Then he helped J.B. sit up.

"Listen up, pal." He shook his friend's shoulders with affection. "You must have rocks in your head. Virtual rocks. 'Cause I'm not going anywhere without you."

J.B. nodded, acknowledging their friendship with a grateful look. Words were not needed.

An explosion rocked the sky overhead.

V.R. Ryan shielded his friend as sizzling fragments pelted them. Then he looked around for some kind of cover. They were near the edge of a rocky quarry. That would have to do.

V.R. Ryan helped J.B. run a little farther. Then he settled him in a small cove behind a boulder. "We'd better hold up for a minute," Trooper Ryan said.

"Thanks," J.B. gasped. "I need a breather."

V.R. Ryan glanced back at the mutants. What would their next move be?

From a distance, Battlebot saw the Troopers stopping. He saw that J.B. was nearly finished. And he knew that Trooper Ryan would never leave his friend behind.

Battlebot had an idea. An idea that would make him look good in Grimlord's eyes. He stopped the other robots from advancing.

"Hold it, you worthless drones." He saw that the Troopers were cornered. They would not last long. Anyone could easily capture them now. But Battlebot was selfish and vain. He wanted this moment of glory all to himself.

"Grimlord left me in charge," he growled at the horde. "I shall be the one to destroy the Troopers now that we finally have them pinned down. Now, go. Go! Get back to the dungeon at once!"

The hodgepodge mob of mutant robots were clearly unhappy. They jeered and grumbled their complaints. But Battlebot stood firm. And at last the other robots wandered back to the dungeon, griping in disappointment.

Battlebot grinned. Ah, the satisfaction of using power to one's advantage. This would be the greatest day of his virtual existence!

Battlebot turned back to his pitiful prey. "You are mine, Steel!" he shouted up into the rocks. "Face it. You and your friend are finished!"

With a battle cry, the mutant robot charged wildly toward the quarry, toward Trooper Ryan and J.B.

V.R. Ryan peered down from the rocks. "Wait here," he told J.B. "I have some important business to take care of."

"Careful," J.B. cautioned. "This 'bot's bad news, man."

J.B. leaned back against the boulder and watched his best friend head out—alone— onto the field of battle.

He hated being helpless like this! I'll make it up to you, Trooper Ryan. And that's a promise, he silently pledged to his buddy. That is . . . if we ever get out of this alive.

*A*ll alone, metalbrain?" Trooper Ryan taunted as he leaped out into Battlebot's path.

Battlebot stumbled, but recovered quickly. "I won't need any help taking you down," he said with a sneer. He yanked out his sword. Its wicked blade flashed. "After you've tasted my sword," Battlebot added, "you'll wish you'd never come looking for your friend." Battlebot was not particularly good at strategy. He simply charged forward.

V.R. Ryan easily flipped out of his path.

With an embarrassed snarl, Battlebot whirled around and tossed explosive crescents at the Trooper.

V.R. Ryan dodged them or batted them aside.

Battlebot seethed and charged forward again, sword raised over his head.

V.R. Ryan, weaponless, was poised and ready.

In hand-to-hand combat, V.R. Ryan blocked Battlebot's sword arm with mesmerizing karate blocks. Still, the robot would not give up.

At last V.R. Ryan knocked the sword from Battlebot's hand. It clattered across the rocky ground.

"Way to go, Trooper!" J.B. shouted from the safety of the rocks.

"Clever move, Steel," Battlebot said nastily. "But I've got more weapons where that came from." Battlebot produced an odd wicked-looking hooked weapon. He charged at the Trooper and struck.

"Aaaagh!" V.R. Ryan cried as he absorbed the blow. But he recovered quickly and dodged another strike.

Battlebot seemed tireless. He pressed forward, striking again and again. Finally another blow connected, and V.R. Ryan stumbled back. He fell on the ground beside Battlebot's sword.

"Hey, try a taste of your own sword, 'Bot," V.R. Ryan jeered. He flung the sword at Battlebot.

But the robot batted it away. Battlebot stopped a moment, to enjoy his advantage. The end was now close at hand.

Back in the lab Kaitlin watched the battle on the computer screen, barely breathing. When she saw Battlebot tower over V.R. Ryan, she grabbed the computer and shook it.

"Come on, Trooper Ryan!" she shouted. "You can take him."

Professor Hart looked on with concern.

Jeb barked frantically.

Trooper Ryan had to get up!

V.R. Ryan lay still, waiting for Battlebot to come closer. He thought he heard someone shouting his name. J.B.? Kaitlin? It didn't matter. Somehow he knew his friends were with him in spirit. That thought gave him strength.

Battlebot stepped closer. He loomed over V.R. Ryan, ready to strike.

At just the right moment, V.R. Ryan jumped to his feet and leapt through the air. His internal engine energized as he soared into space. With incredible power, he landed a kick in Battlebot's chest that sent the mutant flying.

The robot exploded in a searing ball of flame.

Back in the lab, Kaitlin cheered and punched the air. Jeb was turning circles and barking wildly.

"Way to go, Trooper!" Kaitlin shouted.

"He's totally virtual!" Jeb agreed with a delighted wagging of his tail.

Professor Hart just nodded. Kaitlin wondered what he was thinking. She couldn't quite tell by looking at the monitor.

At the edge of the quarry, J.B. smiled as his friend returned and helped him to his feet.

J.B. shook his head. "You were awesome, man! Simply awesome!"

V.R. Ryan grinned. "Let's get you out of here before we run into any more trouble." He put his arm around his best friend and helped him to his feet.

Time to get back home to the real world.

"We had them in our hands! And you let them get away?"

Grimlord had conveniently returned to his dungeon—now that all the fighting was over. And he was making up for lost time with his shouting.

Grimlord was definitely displeased with the way his robots had handled things while he was gone. The business takeovers he'd handled as Karl Ziktor while back in the real world were not enough to help his mood. "You're worthless! All of you!"

His mutant robots moaned and trembled in fear. Many scurried into the dark corners of the dungeon to hide from their master's fury.

In a blind rage Grimlord clenched his fist so tightly it glowed a fiery red.

"Next time, Troopers, you're mine! And next time, I won't let these idiot robots allow you to slip away!"

16

CHAPTER

*A*re you sure this is going to work, Professor?" Kaitlin asked anxiously.

Ryan, transformed back into his real-world self, was with J.B. and Kaitlin back in Professor Hart's secret laboratory. They were trying to restore J.B.'s damaged powers.

Kaitlin gently held J.B.'s hand and helped him lie back on the table.

Ryan was right by his side. "Yeah, Professor. We need J.B. and his virtualizer back at full strength."

Professor Hart mumbled to himself while his eyes scanned the room. "Yes, well, let's see," he said at last. "I'm familiar with the process Grimlord used to rob J.B. of his powers. . . ."

Ryan, Kaitlin, Jeb, and especially J.B. looked at the professor expectantly.

"Let me see now," he went on. "If I can just remember how to reverse amplification of his bipolar attributes . . ."

"Uh-oh," Jeb said with a worried yelp. "Sounds negative, J.B."

"That's it!" the professor exclaimed. He started laughing.

The Troopers glanced at each other with worried frowns.

"Negative. Negative!" the professor repeated. "Negative polarities! Thanks, Jeb."

Jeb barked happily and wagged his tail.

"Now," Professor Hart continued. "Get set, everyone. I'm ready to proceed. Um-hmm, this should work . . . I think."

J.B. cocked an eyebrow and smiled at his friends. "Uh, better wish me luck, guys," he said with a shaky laugh.

Kaitlin and Ryan gave J.B. a thumbs-up sign and stepped away from the table.

Sometimes Professor Hart's ways could shake a person up, J.B. thought with a shake of his head. Especially when it came to a serious experiment like this. But in the long run, they all trusted the gifted scientist. J.B.

chuckled. I guess I don't really have much choice!

Professor Hart began the process. "Here we go, everybody. . . ."

J.B. was suddenly struck by a beam of light from above. His entire body, head to toe, began to glow mysteriously.

Kaitlin and Ryan jumped. They tried not to look too worried.

Jeb lay down, covered his eyes with his paws, and began to howl forlornly. "I can't look! Let me know when it's all over!" he moaned.

The seconds crawled by as they watched the mysterious light envelop their friend.

J.B. didn't move a muscle. He could have been asleep. Or—

CLICK! The beam stopped, and the light faded.

Ryan and Kaitlin waited a few seconds. When nothing happened, they rushed to their friend's side.

"J.B.!" Ryan cried. "Are you OK?"

Slowly J.B opened his eyes. He lay very still a moment, blinking. Then slowly he sat up. He just rested there a few seconds, then swung his feet off the side.

"J.B.!" cried Kaitlin. "Speak to us. Are you all right?"

"I . . . I don't know," J.B. answered.

Slowly he stood. He cast his friends a worried look. "Let me see."

Kaitlin and Ryan watched, breathless.

Even Professor Hart seemed a little worried.

Then suddenly J.B. let loose. He kicked, punched, and chopped his way through a series of highly skilled karate moves. He ended with a flying kick—and a grin.

Jeb barked happily. "I'd say he's back on his feet, man."

"Yes," Professor Hart added. "And according to my calculations and readings, all his V.R. powers are restored as well."

J.B. turned to the screen with a great big smile. "Thanks, Professor."

"My pleasure," the professor responded affectionately.

Then J.B. turned to Ryan. "You risked your life coming into Grimlord's dungeon after me. You didn't have to do that. And I'm never going to forget it."

"Hey," Ryan said, shrugging. "What are friends for?"

J.B. grinned. Then his face became serious. "There's only one thing bothering me."

"What?" Ryan asked.

"While I was in Grimlord's dungeon, I heard him talking with his generals," J.B. said. "I couldn't hear them well, so I'm not really sure what they're planning. But I have a feeling that Grimlord has another trick up his sleeve."

"Hmmm," Ryan said. "And I'm sure they're planning to play it on us."

He placed a hand on Kaitlin's and J.B.'s shoulders. "Heads up, Troopers. Whatever Grimlord's planning, we've got to be ready."

SWOOSH! Ryan carved a fast wide turn on his in-line skates He stopped to tighten his helmet strap, then streaked down the curving paved walkway.

"Now!" Gathering himself up, he soared over a park bench, then landed on the other side in a soft crouch.

Not bad, he told himself as he rolled to a stop. Could have jumped higher. Could have landed smoother.

He turned around and headed back up the inclining pavement with a determined grin. Good job, Ryan. Now, let's try it again.

It was a beautiful sunny day in Cross World City. Ryan and J.B. had taken off an hour to come here, throw on their skates and protective gear, and practice their jumps and spins.

As the noon hour arrived, the park began to fill with midday joggers, lunchers, nannies, and college students. Everyone seemed intent on squeezing all the juice out of this perfect day.

Definitely a day to enjoy the weather and forget your troubles, Ryan thought. Virtual or not!

J.B. and Ryan had made a pact: They promised not to talk about a certain mutant leader. Not even to think about what plans he might be stirring up. At least for a little while.

"Hey, Ryan," J.B. called. He dragged his heel and spun to a stop. "I think we forgot something."

"Yeah?" Ryan asked, skating circles around his friend. "Like what?"

"Weren't we supposed to meet Kaitlin for lunch?" J.B. asked.

Ryan stumbled to a stop. He checked his watch. "Oh, man!" he said, smacking his helmet. "You're right. Race you there?"

"You're on!" cried J.B.

The two friends charged off across the park.

Ten minutes later, neck and neck, they arrived at the offices of the *Underground*.

"I won!" J.B. cried, arms raised overhead.

"You lost!" Ryan said.

They eyed each other in friendly rivalry.

"A tie," Ryan said at last.

"OK," said J.B. "We'll *call* it a tie."

Both guys laughed as they opened the door the *Underground* and rolled inside. Usually the newspaper was a pretty casual office. No one batted an eye when two guys in helmets, kneepads, and skates zoomed through the room.

But today things looked different. The newsroom was packed and noisy. Reporters dashed about the room, typed frantically at their computers, talked into phones.

Kaitlin glanced up as the guys rolled around her desk.

"Hey, Kaitlin," Ryan said. "Ready for lunch?"

"Hey, you!" Woody rushed up to Ryan and J.B. "We're on a deadline here! Why aren't you writing something?"

"Well, uh . . . we don't work here," J.B. said.

"That's no excuse!" Woody shouted. He paused and scratched his head. "At least, I don't think so. . . ." Then he dashed over to another reporter's desk and began to discuss a story, frantically waving his hands.

Kaitlin looked a little frenzied, too. "Aren't you guys a bit early?" she said, still involved with her work.

Ryan and J.B. looked at their watches, and each other, and shrugged.

"Can we help out?" Ryan asked.

Kaitlin smiled. "Just hang on. We've got a couple of minutes before—"

RIIIIINNNNNNGGGGGG!

Kaitlin gasped at the sound of a bell.

Across the room Woody shouted, *"Crashing!"*

Ryan and J.B. looked on, amazed, as total panic swept the newsroom.

Reporters frantically jabbed at their computer keyboards. Everyone was talking and shouting.

Kaitlin urgently typed in a command, over and over. Each time she shook her head in frustration.

Woody had been dashing around the room. Now he grabbed the phone on the corner of Kaitlin's desk and jabbed in some numbers. After a moment's wait, he quickly began shouting questions.

What in the world is going on? Ryan wondered.

Suddenly every single computer in the room flickered . . . and then went blank.

"The stories . . ." Kaitlin gasped. She hammered a key in vain. "Gone. Everything's gone."

J.B. wheeled around her desk. He pulled off his helmet. "Let me try."

Kaitlin gave up her seat and let J.B. take over. He typed at the keyboard, trying every trick he knew. At last he looked up at Kaitlin. "A computer virus has entered the system and wiped out all the *Underground*'s computers."

Woody slowly hung up the phone. He looked at Kaitlin and her friends in amazement. "I can't believe it. Every single computer in Cross World City has been knocked out!"

Eyes a little glazed, Woody wandered off to tell the rest of the staff what had happened.

"If the computers are down all over," J.B. said with a worried frown, "then the ones in the lab might be down, too!"

Ryan looked at his friends in alarm. "The professor!"

The V.R. Troopers had no idea what would happen to the holographic existence of Professor Hart if his computer shut down.

Without another word, Ryan, Kaitlin, and J.B. ran for the door.

Karl Ziktor was channel surfing on his giant-screen office TV.

CLICK.

A close-up of a blank computer screen on Channel 7.

CLICK.

A frantic newscaster on Channel 13.

CLICK.

Even PBS had shut down its children's programming with a special news bulletin.

Ziktor had activated the mute button so he couldn't hear what any of the reporters were saying. But he didn't need to hear. He knew.

After all, hadn't he made it all happen?

Every single computer in Cross World City had crashed. Business and industry had been shut down. But to Ziktor, those were only the comic side effects.

Ziktor laid down the channel changer and picked up Juliet. He stroked her cold skin and congratulated himself. His brilliant plan was working perfectly.

An assistant knocked and entered. She looked like an ordinary office assistant in a nice business suit and stylishly cropped hair. But her words were far from ordinary.

"Your virus has entered Professor Hart's computer system," she reported. "We will have complete control."

"Excellent," Ziktor drawled. "Now leave me."

The assistant backed out and firmly shut the door.

Ziktor gave Juliet a little pat good-bye. Then his arm snaked out to the corner of his desk. His hand enveloped the icy curve of his crystal energy sphere.

"Forces of darkness, empower me!" he called. "Take me back to my virtual reality!"

The flashes of lightning reflected on the huge glass windows. Ziktor began his transformation. Once more, he was turning into Grimlord, master of the virtual world.

"With my specially designed computer virus, I'll soon have access to all the secrets in Professor Hart's laboratory," he gloated. "And then," he added just before he completely disappeared, "I'll destroy the V.R. Troopers once and for all!"

*J*eb was laughing his head off. "Th-th-th-th-that's all, folks!" he howled, then giggled hysterically.

Ryan, Kaitlin, and J.B. stood in the doorway to the lab with open-mouthed stares.

Every screen in the lab was lit up with cartoons?

Not a good sign, Ryan thought.

"Jeb," Ryan asked nervously. "Where's the professor?"

"Adios, amigos," Jeb answered. "He's outta here!"

Quickly the three Troopers dashed for the console. They tried to restore the lab's computer systems. Nothing J.B. did seemed to work.

At last the cartoons vanished.

"Aw, shucks!" Jeb complained.

They all waited for the professor's thoughtful face to appear. But there was nothing. Nothing but a snowy hissing screen.

J.B. kept working, trying things. "I can't find the professor on any of the systems," he said. He cast his friends a nervous glance. "I . . . I hope the virus hasn't deleted him."

"Virus!" Jeb cried. "Hey, stand back, everybody!"

Ryan smiled. "Not that kind of virus, Jeb. A computer virus is a program that destroys other people's data. It wiped out all the stories at Kaitlin's paper."

"Let's try a memory search," J.B. suggested.

Ryan brought over the V.R. visors and passed them out. "We'll monitor the search with these."

The Troopers put their visors on. They waited expectantly.

"Oh, man!" Ryan gasped.

"Weird," Kaitlin said.

This time they saw no lights, colors, or dramatic images, only a vast white nothingness.

J.B. kept working. "Hang on a minute," he mumbled.

Ryan and Kaitlin both held their breath.

"OK," J.B. said at last. "Activating search . . . now!"

"Huh!" Ryan gasped.

The Troopers jerked back from a flash of bright light. Then bold startling images rushed past them. The visors were enabling them to witness the computer's rapid-fire search through its files. Ground battles, explosions, data, and diaries blurred past them.

And then . . . "Found him!" J.B. cried.

He struck a button and waited.

Professor Hart's face appeared.

"All right!" Ryan shouted.

"Yes!" Kaitlin joined in.

What a relief to have the professor back! Ryan thought.

As they all settled down, however, Ryan noticed that the professor looked a little different. His face appeared a lot larger than usual, almost completely filling the screen. And he did not look happy.

"Well, if it isn't the V.R. Troopers," he said flatly.

The Troopers pulled off their visors and smiled at Professor Hart.

"Professor," said Ryan, "a virus has entered the lab's computers. It's still there, infecting all the programs. But at least it hasn't affected you."

"This information is useless!" Professor Hart cried. "You are wasting my time."

Ryan gasped in surprise.

"What's wrong with him?" Kaitlin whispered.

"I don't know," J.B. said to the side. "It's like he got up on the wrong side of the microchip."

Hmmm, Ryan thought. Odd.

But then again, the professor existed as a holographic computer image. And the system he lived in had just gone through a major shakeup. I guess that would be enough to put just about anybody in a bad mood, Ryan mused.

To Grimlord, the V.R. Troopers were even more funny than cartoons. "They don't even suspect the virus is mine!" he crowed. "They could never guess where it's coming from: my secret underwater military station. They'll never find it!"

Grimlord waved his wand. A blast of light shot out, creating a shimmering picture.

First he and his robots saw an underwater military complex.

Then the image changed to a view of the inside. The place was filled with skugs and mutant robots.

"General Ivar, Colonel Iceborg," Grimlord called. "Report!"

"Success, Your Lordship," Ivar said. "We are transmitting the virus directly into Hart's lab."

"Yes," Iceborg said excitedly. "We control the professor's image!"

Grimlord was delighted. "And with his image," he said, "I will now be able to control the V.R. Troopers."

Back in the lab a long string of numbers filed across the bottom of the computer screen. It looked like the stock market report that always ran across the bottom of the picture on the 24-hour news channel.

The Troopers listened carefully to the professor as he explained. "There's a break in the reality barrier at this location," he told them. "Prepare for virtual combat!"

J.B. started to type on the keyboard. "I'll confirm it."

"Don't question me!" the professor snapped. "Go! I will take care of bringing the lab's computers back on-line while you are gone."

The Troopers looked at one another confusedly. The professor sure was acting cranky.

Maybe it has something to do with the computer problems, Kaitlin thought. Maybe holographic computer images have their bad days, too.

"OK, Professor," Ryan said at last. "We'll go."

With a brief wave, the Troopers left the laboratory.

The portal whooshed closed.

For a moment all was silent in the white modern lab. Then the image of Professor Hart laughed. "Yes, my Troopers, travel to your virtual doom!" he said.

"Whoa," Jeb said, a little confused. "That sounds bogus."

"Get back, you flea-infested mutt!" the professor shouted.

Jeb cowered and stepped away, his tail between his legs. "Yow, that hurts."

Professor Hart glared at him silently.

Jeb growled. Something smells a little fishy in this lab, the bloodhound thought. I'd better keep my eyes and ears open while the Troopers are gone.

*T*he Troopers flew down the road in Kaitlin's red sports car.

The professor's voice came to them over a laptop computer connected to the car's cellular phone. "The reality break should be just about there."

The car came to a bend in the road. Up ahead was a stalled car, its hood and trunk raised. Four men in business suits stood by the car looking helpless.

Kaitlin slowed her car to a halt.

"Why are you stopping!" the professor cried angrily.

"Professor," Kaitlin answered, "we don't see a break. There's nothing here but a stalled car and four men in suits."

"Keep going," the professor said impatiently. "The break will occur directly before you!"

"We can't do that right now," J.B. said. "If we do, Grimlord's mutants will be right on top of those people!"

"Listen, Professor," Ryan said. "We're going to try to help these people and get them out of here first."

Ryan, J.B., and Kaitlin climbed out of the car.

"You folks need some help?" Kaitlin called out with a friendly smile.

"Yeah," J.B. said. "We're pretty good mechanics."

The businessmen stared blankly.

The three friends looked at one another uneasily.

Ryan tried again. "We'd be happy to lend you a hand. . . . Or maybe not!" he suddenly shouted.

The businessmen turned into skugs!

Two of the mutants crouched in front of them while the other pair made a fast break around the sides. Surrounded, Kaitlin, Ryan, and J.B. turned their backs to each other and faced out from the center.

"Ready!" shouted Kaitlin. The three friends adopted a bent-knee stance.

"Aim!" J.B. cried. Their hands rose at once to fighting positions.

"Fire!" yelled Ryan. Like spring-loaded darts, they sprang apart and flew into the faces of the skugs.

"HI-YAH!" Kaitlin's heel shot against one skug's chest, flipping him over backward.

Another skug doubled over as Ryan landed a punch to its middle. Then it rolled head over heels when Ryan's foot slammed from behind.

J.B.'s kick to the chest drove another skug backward over Kaitlin. She crouched, then sprang up, flipping the mutant into the path of another charging skug.

The two creatures crashed into each other, short-circuited, and disappeared.

Together the Troopers knocked the last two skugs back against their car. Kaitlin and J.B. took up position on either side, like bookends. Ryan faced them from the middle.

The Troopers pressed in on the skugs. And with three final chops, they smashed the skugs together. The mutants vanished in a short-circuiting flash.

Ryan, J.B., and Kaitlin paused to catch their breath.

The sounds of struggle had disappeared, replaced by birdsong and leaves rustling in the breeze. The stalled car was abandoned.

J.B. looked around, puzzled. "There's still no sign of a break in the reality barrier here."

Ryan put his hands on his hips, thinking. "J.B., could the virus have caused some kind of system error in the computer?"

"I don't know," J.B. replied. "But we'd better find out."

*C*ross World City could have been called Grimlord City the next day—with the emphasis on *grim*.

The whole city was in complete chaos. Business came to a screeching halt. Ordinary daily life had been stirred up like a tossed salad.

People were stunned. They couldn't do their work. They couldn't even buy a postage stamp, because the post office's new computerized stamp machines were shut down.

When had they all gotten so dependent on computers? It had happened without them even noticing.

In spite of the trouble, the V.R. Troopers were forced to split up for a while. They all had other commitments, things in the real world that needed to be done.

Ryan, Kaitlin, and J.B. were the kind of people who showed up when they said they would. Who did what they promised. Besides, they had to go on with their normal lives in order to keep their Trooper identities a secret.

Kaitlin had to get back to the *Underground* and finish her stories for the next edition. With computers down all over Cross World City, it was even more important to get out the news. And it would take twice as long to do everything—writing, editing, ad sales, and production—without computers.

Ryan had classes to teach at Tao Dojo. Some of the younger kids were really upset. They'd heard a lot of mixed-up talk about viruses and crashes in the past few hours. Grown-ups everywhere—at home, at school, in stores— were acting frantic and weird.

Ryan used his classes that day to help the kids calm down.

I know what it's like to be young and scared, like these kids, he thought. I felt helpless when I lost Dad.

Learning karate had helped Ryan feel strong in a scary, unpredictable world.

So today he shared with his students a special lesson—something his father had taught him: To conquer fear of the unknown, concentrate on the known.

Ryan guided his students through movements that they knew by heart. Step by step. Slow and sure. By the end of the class, many of the kids were even smiling again.

J.B. was at the dojo today, too. He was trying to get the computer up and running again. He had worked pretty hard to set up Tao's business on the computer, and now all his work was lost. He got nothing but gibberish on the screen.

Tao looked over J.B.'s shoulder. "Is there a problem?" he asked.

"I'm not sure," J.B. answered, frustrated. "It's going to take a while before I can get back on-line and recreate the school's financial accounts. Either that or look for the old backup disks."

Tao nodded. He had not developed an affection for computers yet. He much preferred his ancient abacus, with its rows of colored wooden beads for counting. No batteries or electricity needed.

Tao had a class of students arriving, so he plodded off, leaving the computer problems in J.B.'s capable hands.

As soon as he left, J.B. slipped the V.R. disk into the computer. Then he looked up as Kaitlin rushed in.

"J.B.," she said, flopping down in a chair next to him. "Something weird's going on. Our sources at the paper say that no one entered the virus into the computers. It just appeared out of the datasphere—by itself!"

"A virtual virus?" J.B. exclaimed. "Hey, we definitely need the professor to help us out with this."

J.B. typed quickly. Kaitlin leaned forward to watch.

Ryan had just finished teaching his last karate class, and came in to see what was up with his friends.

Right away he sensed a problem.

For some reason they weren't getting through to the professor. Suddenly J.B. let out a long whistle.

Ryan and Kaitlin leaned forward to read what the computer said: "Pathway inoperative."

"Uh-oh," J.B. moaned. "We're in real trouble!"

"Pathway inoperative?" Ryan asked. "What does that mean?"

J.B. spun around in his chair. He shook his head as if he couldn't believe what he was thinking. "If the computer pathways are down, the professor can't talk to us. Here *or* at the lab!"

"What?" Ryan cried.

"Then who's using the professor's image?" Kaitlin said.

But as soon as the words were out of her mouth, they knew. They all knew.

Ryan said it aloud: "Grimlord."

BEEP!

J.B. swung back around to the computer. He read the words that had just appeared on the screen.

"Pathway operative."

J.B. shook his head. "Weird! The pathway works now!" He tapped on the keyboard a few moments.

Suddenly Professor Hart appeared on the screen. At least it looked like Professor Hart. The image had the same face and hair. The shirt was identical. And the eyes looked familiar, didn't they?

"Grimlord is attacking!" the professor announced to the Troopers. "You must enter virtual reality! Find out where the virus

111

transmission site is and destroy it!" His voice sounded the same, too. Pretty much.

"Uh, just a minute, Professor," J.B. said. "We've got some static. Hold on." J.B. pressed a key on the keyboard. Then he turned to his friends, his dark eyes troubled. "He can't hear us now."

Kaitlin leaned forward. "Is that really the professor?" she asked softly.

"Or is it Grimlord?" Ryan wondered aloud.

J.B. entered some additional commands on the computer. He shook his head. "Whoever it is, he's using the professor's path." He shrugged. "All I can say for sure, guys, is that it could be the professor."

Ryan leaned forward, elbows on his knees, hands clasped before him. How could they be sure what to do?

They could stay where they were and do nothing. They could wait. See what developed. That would be the safest thing to do. At least for now.

Listen to me! Ryan thought. Talking about what's safe for us and what isn't when the whole world is at risk!

Safety was important when it came to seat belts and front door locks and practicing martial arts. But when it came to stopping Grimlord and his virtual army, personal safety was low on the list. Ryan couldn't risk the lives of millions of people because he was afraid of taking action.

Ryan made his decision. "If there's a chance this is really the professor," he said, "we have to take the risk."

Ryan and Kaitlin thought a moment about what Ryan was saying. Then they solemnly agreed.

The three teens slipped out a side door and out into the back alley. They took out their transformation pendants, the ones the *real* Professor Hart had given them. Together they raised their pendants to the sky.

"Trooper transform!" they shouted.

Powerful blue lightning rocketed from the jewels set into the pendants' core. A sound like electronic feedback on an amplifier rang in their ears. And Ryan, Kaitlin, and J.B. transformed in a shattering of colored light. The ordinary teenagers were now powerful V.R. Troopers!

With a shout they were leaping into the sky toward the huge Mothership that would enable them to travel between the worlds of reality and virtual reality. A hatch opened on the bottom of the ship, and they hurtled inside, down long twisting corridors of flashing blinking lights, till they plopped into their seats in the cockpit.

"OK, Professor," Trooper J.B. announced, hoping like mad that he was addressing the real one. "We're ready!"

The Mothership tore upward into the sky. The Troopers settled into their mission as Professor Hart's image flickered onto the cockpit's computer screen.

"To find Grimlord's hidden base," he told them, "we need readings from both the virtual world and the real world. Troopers Ryan and Kaitlin, take the ship into virtual reality. Trooper J.B., you remain in the real world."

"Acknowledged," V.R. Ryan answered.

But V.R. Kaitlin shook her head. "I don't like splitting up like this, guys," she whispered. "Especially not now, with everything so uncertain."

"I understand," V.R. Ryan said. "But it's the only way to find the base."

Kaitlin sighed, then nodded her agreement. "Take care, Trooper J.B."

"Don't worry," Trooper J.B. answered confidently. "I'll stay in touch."

With a whoosh, Trooper J.B. exited the ship. Minutes later he landed solidly below on a cliffside in the wilderness. "I'm in position, Trooper Ryan," he reported.

"We read you," V.R. Ryan answered.

Trooper J.B. looked up into the cloudless blue sky. The majestic Mothership seemed to hover in the air for a moment.

"We'll be back for you as soon as possible," V.R. Ryan called down.

And then in a flash, the Mothership slipped from the real world.

"Take all the time you want," Grimlord muttered from his throne in his virtual dungeon. "No need to rush back at all. Take my word for it." He laughed aloud. "After all, why bother? By the time you return to reality, your friends will no longer be there!"

*T*rooper J.B. stood on the high, windy cliff-side waiting for something, anything, to happen.

And something was going to happen, he could sense it. He almost wished for it to hurry. For he could not do battle with something he couldn't see, something looming just out of sight in the future.

In his virtual form, V.R. J.B.'s powers were outrageous. But he always felt better when he and the other two Troopers could face the danger together.

He and his friends each had their special talents. Each was talented in his or her own way. As a Trooper, V.R. J.B. felt strong. As part of the V.R. team, he felt invincible.

He remembered something Tao had taught them. Tao's philosophy of the martial arts was simple. They were a weapon for defense. He did not believe at all in the strategy that the guy with the biggest gun wins.

One day J.B. and his friends had gone on a picnic in the country with Tao. After a huge meal, they sat around talking and enjoying the sunshine.

Then Tao had abruptly stood up. He had walked around gathering an armload of sticks. Then he sat back down on their blanket.

He gave each of the young people a stick. Each was about as big around as a hockey puck.

"Break the stick," Tao had said.

Ryan, Kaitlin, and J.B. had looked at each other. What was their *sensei* up to now?

"Break the stick," Tao had repeated.

"Easy," Ryan had said.

Each of them had easily broken the stick in two.

"Nothing to it," J.B. had said with a grin.

Then Tao gave three sticks to each person.

"Break the sticks," Tao had repeated.

Ryan had glanced at the others. He held the three sticks together and tried to break them.

He couldn't.

He tried to break them across his knee. Ouch! He still couldn't break the sticks.

Neither could Kaitlin or J.B.

"Anybody got a chainsaw?" J.B. had joked.

Tao smiled. "Alone"—he snapped one stick in two—"you break." Then he held three sticks in a bundle. "Together"—he tried to break the sticks and failed—"together you are strong."

J.B. still had those three sticks. He kept them on a bookshelf in his room at home.

So he would never forget.

A vague metallic clanking behind V.R. J.B. made the hair stand up on the back of his neck. He got the feeling he was about to get his wish. Something was about to happen. He spun around.

In the distance he spotted Grimlord's mutant soldier Metaborg, a squat, low-to-the-ground robot. The mutant was slowly but steadily approaching

Then, through his helmet screen, V.R. J.B. could see that Metaborg was about to attack.

V.R. J.B. drew first and fired.

The shot struck the top of Metaborg in a shower of sparks. It stumbled but did not fall.

V.R. J.B. backed off. He pulled out his light rod and waited.

The strange robot's head rose taller several inches up out of its body. It was going to fire again.

Acting fast, Trooper J.B. jumped into the air as a lightning bolt flashed. Tumbling away, he saw rocks explode on the ground where he'd just been standing. Recovering quickly, he got to his feet. So far so good, he thought. He kept his eyes glued to the robot, watching for the next shot. A sound overhead distracted him. He glanced up quickly.

"Oh, great!" he muttered.

Incoming enemy airships were zooming toward him like flies to a pie. Except these flies attacked with deadly fire.

Trooper J.B. began to run toward the cover of the trees. The ground around him plowed up from enemy fire.

Then the Trooper disappeared in the smoke.

*T*rooper Ryan!" Kaitlin exclaimed as she sat at the controls in the cockpit of the Mothership. They were traveling through virtual reality trying to discover where the computer virus was coming from.

"What is it?" V.R. Ryan demanded. "What's wrong?"

V.R. Kaitlin furiously entered commands on the control panel's computer keyboard. But the answer came up the same, again and again.

Keeping her eyes on the screen, she reported, "I'm not detecting the computer virus on any of the virtual frequencies."

V.R. Ryan checked his controls. Then he gasped in surprise. "No wonder you can't get any readings," he said. "Our signals are being jammed. . . ." He ran a check to find the source of the problem. What was going on? Who was doing this!

Seconds ticked by like hours.

At last his computer locked on to the answer. "Kaitlin! You won't believe this!" he cried. "The frequency jamming our signals is coming from Professor Hart's lab!"

He and V.R. Kaitlin stared at each other. Realization washed over them like a cold, wet mist.

V.R. Ryan spoke aloud what they were both thinking. "Trooper Kaitlin! That Professor Hart who sent us here on this mission—he's a fake!"

V.R. Kaitlin nodded miserably. "We should have known!"

V.R. Ryan pounded the arm of his seat with his fist. "The whole thing was a complete setup. It's a trap!"

"And we left Trooper J.B.—back in the real world—all alone!" V.R. Kaitlin said.

V.R. Ryan turned back to the Mothership's controls. "We've got to get back to him—right away."

Just then they picked up a distress signal. It was coming from the real world.

"Hey, Troopers," they heard V.R. J.B. calling. "I could use some help here!"

"We read you, Trooper!" V.R. Ryan answered. "Hold on!"

The Troopers' hands flew over the controls. The Mothership turned and headed back.

V.R. Kaitlin flipped the proper controls, preparing the ship for the switch. Then she announced: "Reentering reality . . . now!"

The Mothership hummed as it passed the virtual barrier. Soon it appeared again in the real sky.

"Look!" V.R. Kaitlin cried, pointing ahead of them in the sky.

A swarm of airbots was attacking the ground. They were flying back and forth right above the area where Troopers Ryan and Kaitlin had left Trooper J.B.

V.R. Ryan aimed the Mothership's guns. He fired. The blast struck the front ship. And the airbot exploded in the sky.

"Maybe that will discourage the rest of them," V.R. Ryan said.

The airbots veered away. But V.R. J.B. was not out of danger yet.

Down on the ground Trooper J.B. was once again going one-on-one with Grimlord's robot Metaborg.

But now the squat robot was changing. Within seconds it grew into a tall humanoid-like robot.

V.R. J.B. raised his light rod, ready for the attack. They sparred a few moments as skugs appeared out of nowhere. The skugs surrounded the fighters, cheering on the anvil-headed robot.

Back in the secret lab, the image of Professor Hart appeared on the screen. Beside his face a digital clock face ticked, counting down the seconds.

Three minutes left on the timer.

Three minutes until what? Jeb wondered as he sprawled on the cool lab floor and watched. Dinner, I hope!

So far things were pretty boring around the lab today, the dog thought with a pout. He wished the weird professor would show more cartoons.

Suddenly Jeb sat up. He was speechless—which hadn't happened much at all since he'd gotten the ability to talk.

He spotted V.R. J.B. on one of the screens. These are definitely not home videos, Jeb thought. J.B. was being attacked by one of Grimlord's mutant robots!

The professor glared down at the stunned dog. "In just moments, the Troopers will be destroyed, my mangy mutt! Then I will possess the secret of mass inter-reality travel."

"Prof," Jeb said, cocking his head to one side. "You've short-circuited, man! Like, you've blown a fuse or something!"

Professor Hart roared with laughter.

Man, he is really losing it! Jeb thought.

Then the professor's face wavered on the screen. Something was happening. His face was changing. . . . Jeb had never seen the old guy look like this before! What was going on?

Jeb yelped worriedly as the face began to take on a familiar look. "Uh-oh. Bad news!"

This face he'd been talking to all day—this guy who looked like Professor Hart—wasn't the real Professor Hart at all!

The transformation was completed.

Jeb definitely knew that face: Grimlord! Panting hard, Jeb jumped up onto one of the lab's many control panels. He struck at a button with his right paw.

"Yo, Trooper Ryan! Urgent message! Listen up!" the dog shouted into the intercom system. "The prof is bogus, man!"

V.R. Ryan's voice crackled back over the intercom: "We read you, Jeb. Good boy! Get out of the lab—now!"

"No prob-lem-o!" the dog answered. "I'm outta here. See ya!"

Jeb gave Grimlord one last "GrrrRUFF! GrrrRUFF!" then scampered out through the door.

Grimlord laughed at the ridiculous animal. Good riddance! He hated dogs. He didn't trust them. Too friendly and slobbery. He much preferred collecting a much different sort of pet. Mutant ones. Slimy ones. Maybe even a V.R. Trooper or two . . . ?

Nah. Troopers were more pest than pet, Grimlord decided. Better to exterminate them altogether!

23

CHAPTER

*T*rooper J.B. was holding on as best he could—considering a mutant robot was trying to destroy him, and a wild mob of ugly skugs was cheering the 'bot on.

One of the skugs threw rocks at V.R. J.B., which made him turn around.

Metaborg took the advantage and grabbed V.R. J.B. He held him over his head and flung him back and forth like a rag doll. The skug mob raised dust as it jumped up and down and cheered.

Then the Metaborg hurled V.R. J.B. to the ground.

V.R. J.B. was dazed for a moment. Then he rose up on his elbows and shook his head. His inner circuits sparked. He hoped the Troopers would get there soon.

Up in the Mothership the two other Troopers saw that V.R. J.B. was in trouble.

"Trooper J.B.'s going down!" V.R. Ryan cried.

"I'm on my way," V.R. Kaitlin said.

Down on the ground Metaborg was stalking V.R. J.B. Suddenly the sound of incoming aircraft split the air. The skugs fell back in fear. Metaborg stared up into the sky.

A hatch had opened up in the bottom of the Mothership. Like a surprise from a piñata, V.R. Kaitlin was zooming down in the Troopers' total assault vehicle.

From the cockpit V.R. Kaitlin shouted, "Launching weapons!" Guns appeared on the vehicle. "Fire!" she cried.

Explosions rocked the ground near the scene of the fighting. The mutants skittered back like roaches.

That gave V.R. Kaitlin a little space and time. She programmed the total assault vehicle to hover in position. Then quickly she flew up and out of the cockpit. Seconds later she hit the ground running. Soon she was at V.R.

J.B.'s side. Gently she put her arm around his shoulders and helped him sit up.

"Trooper J.B.," she said urgently. "Can you move?"

"My power's drained somewhat," he said. "I need a recharge."

"You've got it," V.R. Kaitlin said.

The two Troopers touched hands. Energy flowed from V.R. Kaitlin's form into V.R. J.B.'s weakened one, like a rechargeable battery. Seconds later V.R. J.B. was restored to full power.

Just in time! Metaborg was coming after them. The two Troopers drew their weapons and fired. Two flaming blasts streaked out and struck the charging robot. It struggled to stay up.

V.R. J.B. swung his light rod. A writhing ribbon of electricity shot out.

Metaborg crackled loudly and then exploded. Instantly the robot's cheering section disappeared.

"All right!" V.R. Ryan cheered from the cockpit of the Mothership still hovering high in the sky.

"Fool!" he heard someone shout at him.

V.R. Ryan turned to look at his computer screen.

The dark face of Grimlord stared back at him! "Do you think it matters if you destroy one puny worthless robot?" Grimlord asked sarcastically. "All of Professor Hart's laboratory systems are about to come on-line. And when they do, you foolish Trooper, all of reality is mine!"

V.R. Ryan radioed down to the others. "We've got to cut off Grimlord's communication source!"

V.R. J.B. responded. "I'm on my way." He leaped into the total assault vehicle.

V.R. Kaitlin took a running jump and flew back up into the Mothership. Once seated in the cockpit, V.R. Kaitlin went to work. "I've plotted a trajectory from Grimlord's last transmission," she announced. "It looks like a virtual installation."

"Did you hear that, Trooper J.B.?" V.R. Ryan called. "If you destroy it, that should end Grimlord's access to the lab."

Trooper J.B. steered the total assault vehicle for the edges of reality. "I'm entering virtual reality. Preparing for immersion. *Now!*"

The total assault vehicle whizzed into virtual reality. It flew over a vast wilderness as Trooper J.B. sought the location V.R. Kaitlin had given him. As Trooper J.B. lowered the vehicle toward the trees, the bottom opened up. A huge churning drill motored into position.

The total assault vehicle trembled as it plowed into the ground. V.R. J.B. held on tight as it bored steadily into the rocky soil.

The total assault vehicle rocked and jolted. Lights blinked on and off.

Now I know what a mole feels like, Trooper J.B. thought wryly. Then he felt the sensation of jolting loose. He checked his readings. The total assault vehicle was now whisking furiously through water.

Trooper J.B. had discovered a secret underground ocean. The total assault vehicle's drill churned the water like a huge washing machine.

THUNK! The drill struck metal—but kept going. It sounded like an automobile being ground up in a food processor!

The total assault vehicle was boring right through the roof of Grimlord's secret military hideout! Skugs and robots scattered as the building was torn apart. Ocean water gushed everywhere.

"Firing!" V.R. J.B. shouted. The total assault vehicle blasted away.

And the underwater building exploded violently, turning the water into a steaming hot soup of robots, skugs, and computer hardware.

At that exact instant something happened in the cockpit of the Mothership, too. Grimlord vanished from the computer screen.

Troopers Ryan and Kaitlin whooped in victory.

"Got it!" V.R. Ryan cried.

They'd shut down Grimlord's underwater command center. They'd shut down his link to Professor Hart's computers. Just in time.

But Troopers Ryan and Kaitlin both knew there was more to be done. Time to reconnect with V.R. J.B. And then they could all head back to the real world and check on the secret laboratory.

Neither V.R. Ryan nor V.R. Kaitlin spoke aloud what they were both wondering: Would the real Professor Hart be there?

General Ivar had a raging headache that reached into the deepest wires in his brain circuits. Still wobbly and a bit waterlogged from Trooper J.B.'s attack, he stood before Grimlord's throne in his dungeon.

"General Ivar!" Grimlord barked.

"We escaped, Your Highness," the general said. "But I'm afraid I have some bad news. The computer virus was destroyed before we could completely take over the professor's computer systems."

Ivar's voice got soft and tiny. As if that could keep Grimlord from hearing the truth. "We . . . uh, we failed to obtain his secrets about mass inter-reality travel. And the virus"—his voice got so soft even he couldn't hear himself—"took us years to develop. I don't know if we can ever recreate it." He ended with his eyes closed.

"You worthless pile of rust!" Grimlord shrieked. "Everything was set up. It was all going according to plan. We were seconds, mere *seconds*, away from victory! How could you ruin such a perfect plan?"

General Ivar just rattled. He was trembling too hard to speak.

Grimlord seethed and turned his face to the wall. "Failure!" He hated the word more than any other. But the anger churning inside him would be useful. It would fuel his revenge. It would ignite his imagination, spur him on to the creation of a new plan.

And he swore before all the mutant robots who cowered before him: "We are far from finished, Troopers!"

*R*yan and Kaitlin watched and worried silently as J.B. hacked away at the computer keyboard.

They were back in the hidden laboratory. They had retroformed and were dressed in their normal jeans and T-shirts and high-tops. Everything was back to normal. Except, of course, one of the most important things.

Professor Hart's holographic image on the computer.

Kaitlin scratched Jeb behind the ears. He'd never admit it, but she could tell the sad-eyed bloodhound was a little worried, too.

At last J.B. looked up hopefully at his friends. "I've deleted all traces of Grimlord's computer virus from our systems," he said.

"Cross your fingers, guys. This should bring back the professor."

J.B. bit his lip, then punched a key.

Ryan's heart hammered out the seconds as he and his friends waited. Would it work?

"H-hello?" Professor Hart's rumpled image appeared on the screen.

"Professor!" Ryan cried.

"Party, dude!" Jeb cheered, jumping up and down. "You're back!"

"Back . . . ?" The professor peered closer at the Troopers. "Uh, where is it that I've been . . . exactly?"

"Check the extended memory chips, Professor," J.B. suggested.

The professor whirred and clicked a moment. Then his image jumped in surprise. "Oh, my!" he said as he received the data. "Who could have imagined . . . ?"

Ryan wasn't quite sure what it was. But something about the way the professor talked and acted. . . . Well, Ryan knew in his heart that this was the real Professor Hart. And it'll take a whole lot more to fool me again, Ryan promised himself.

Professor Hart seemed to wander a little, taking everything in. Then he looked directly at the V.R. Troopers. "Your self-reliance in this crisis is to be congratulated."

Ryan, Kaitlin, and J.B. grinned.

Jeb barked. "Thanks a heap, Professor!"

"You've demonstrated that you don't always need me to solve your problems," the professor went on. "And you have proved yourselves as true Virtual Reality Troopers!"

That really made everyone smile.

"Thanks, Professor," Ryan said, beaming.

Then the Troopers filled in the professor on some more of the details of their recent adventure. It was important that Professor Hart understand all that Grimlord was capable of doing.

Next they talked over ideas about how to safeguard the lab's computers against future infiltration. J.B. had a lot of ideas. Professor Hart and J.B. talked excitedly about working together to develop a computer vaccine that would stop any future viruses that Grimlord might create.

Then Jeb told Professor Hart about the cool cartoons he'd watched. The professor promised to watch some with him sometime.

At last Kaitlin sighed. "And now I've really got to get back to the real world. I've got a class to get to."

"What kind of class?" Ryan asked.

Kaitlin laughed. "Didn't I tell you? The computer crash at the *Underground* really shook Woody up—bad. So now he's making all his reporters take a class in how to use manual typewriters."

"You mean the kind that don't use electricity?" J.B. asked with a grin.

"Brutal!" Jeb agreed.

"I'd better be going, too," J.B. said. "I have to get Tao's computer back on-line at the dojo." He shot the Troopers a grin. "Whether he likes it or not!"

J.B. and Kaitlin headed for the door.

"See you later, Ryan," Kaitlin called back over her shoulder.

"Hang in there, guys," Ryan said with a wave.

As his friends left, Ryan sat down next to Jeb. "Good dog," Ryan said, scratching that spot behind his ears that Jeb could never quite reach. The smiling dog settled down into a semi-conscious nap.

Deep in thought, Ryan looked around the room, at all the complex computer equipment.

"Is everything all right, Ryan?" the professor asked gently.

"Now it is, Professor," Ryan answered. He'd rescued J.B. from Grimlord's virtual world. He'd helped bring Professor Hart back to his own special place in the real world.

But he couldn't help thinking of one other special person who was still lost to him.

One other special person who might still be a captive in the virtual world.

25

CHAPTER

*R*yan stopped his motorcycle a respectful distance from the temple and cut the motor. He slowly walked up the long paved path, turning up the collar of his black leather jacket against the cool wind. Then he sat down on the worn steps.

The peaceful beauty of this place was in stark contrast to what he and his friends had just gone through. It calmed him just to sit here and meditate for a time.

He stared off in the distance at the skyline of Cross World City. He thought about all the people who worked and lived there. There were thousands upon thousands of them. Sometimes they seemed like faceless crowds.

But each person was as unique as a snowflake. Each was as special as his friends J.B., Kaitlin, Tao, Jeb, and Professor Hart. As special as his father had been.

The inhabitants of Cross World City had no way of knowing the evil that had threatened their happy lives. He was glad that he had once again been able to help keep those lives safe.

Using my powers to save my best friend, and the lives of all these innocent people was exactly what my dad prepared me for all those years ago, he thought. I hope that somehow, Dad, you know how grateful I am for this gift you've left to me.

His father must have given him many presents as a child. But somehow he couldn't remember any of the toys or other material things. But the memories he had given him were precious gifts. They helped him feel close to Tyler Steel, even though his father was gone. Maybe someday he would see his

father again. Then he could really thank him
for all that he'd given a young boy so many
years ago.

"Dad," Ryan said softly into the wind. "I
wish I could get you back as easily as we did
J.B., as easily as we did the professor."

Ryan blinked back tears. "I'm gonna search
every memory, everything you said to me . . .
until I find you."

Till then he would do all he could to use
those gifts, including his V.R. powers, to keep
the world safe from the threat of Grimlord
and his fiendish army.

Inter-reality travel—it was a mind-blowing
concept. But like most scientific discoveries, it
was neither good nor bad on its own. What
was important for the future of the world was
how people would choose to use it. Ryan
knew that he and his friends were a part of
that decision. And he would never back off
from that trust. Just imagine the places they
might go, the things they might do, if he and
his father and his friends could map out that
new world together!

In the light of the setting sun, Ryan once
again moved silently through a series of

karate exercises. To sharpen his skills. To keep his mind and body in balance.

Over and over again he practiced these simple ancient moves, until the colors of sunset dissolved into a starry sky.

He could never stop working toward perfection.

And he must keep himself ready.

For the future.

Always.